I0661886

James Parker

Meditations for the forty days of Lent

.

James Parker

Meditations for the forty days of Lent

ISBN/EAN: 9783741198335

Manufactured in Europe, USA, Canada, Australia, Japa

Cover: Foto ©Andreas Hilbeck / pixelio.de

Manufactured and distributed by brebook publishing software
(www.brebook.com)

James Parker

Meditations for the forty days of Lent

MEDITATIONS

FOR THE

FORTY DAYS OF LENT.

Oxford and London:
JAMES PARKER AND CO.
DUBLIN: HODGES, FOSTER AND CO.
1872.

Printed by James Parker and Co., Crown-yard, Oxford.

PREFATORY NOTICE.

I HAVE read several of the *Meditations for the Forty Days of Lent* contained in this little volume, and feel sure that many others will find their pleasure and profit therein.

RICHARD C. DUBLIN.

PALACE, DUBLIN,
Jan. 24, 1872.

THERE is one omission throughout these short
readings which needs a few words of explanation,—the absence of notes of reference to
quotations. The only excuse to be offered is,
that the Meditations were not originally written
for publication, and only the very few notes of
reference which are given were made at the
time, though care was then taken to mark all
borrowed words. It would now be all-but impossible to supply this omission; but it may,
perhaps, be forgiven in a book which will probably be mostly used (if at all) by the young,
and in which many foot-notes might have rather a distracting tendency, since the readings
are entirely devotional. Only it may be right to
say, that by far the larger number of quotations
are from the writings of those "ancient Fathers"
of undivided Christendom, to whose authority
the English Prayer-book makes frequent appeal.
If the words of others besides these have occa-

sionally been used, though not unmarked, yet without special acknowledgement, their indulgence is very earnestly asked, since any attempt to remedy the deficiency, with only memory as guide, would certainly cause many mistakes.

One word more of explanation, though there have been already too many for anything so short and slight as these readings. The best teachers have advised us to use method in meditation, —dividing it, for instance, into "preparation, considerations, affections, resolutions,"—and it may seem almost wrong to offer anything called "Meditations," in which no such method or divisions are observed; but as they were written at the suggestion of one to whom it was a happiness to owe any duty, they could but be set down in the only way which want of capacity and of training made possible. A more methodical manner is doubtless the best, since it is so much recommended to us, but it will always be difficult (at least to some minds) without the training of early habit. Thought and emotion are so intermingled, they are so all-but simultaneous, that it is difficult to separate them;

"affections" would with some evaporate in the process of dividing them from "considerations." And indeed feeling can no more be expressed in words, than can perfumes which the sun draws from flowers, though there have been those with love so fervent that they have given expression to it in "words that burn."

But a want of method in written meditations will the less matter, because it would indeed be a great loss if any one were to allow the use of even the best books to take the place of real meditation ; for "according as we neglect meditation, so are our prayers imperfect ; meditation being the soul of prayer*." What may have been real meditation to one can only be devout reading to others ; and the most it can do as a help to meditation will be to suggest some line of thought which may be cast into the method already learned, and used with far more of profit than it yielded to the writer. God will give us thoughts and affections if we ask Him, and nothing can take the place of that communion of the soul with Him. We "cannot

* Bp. Jeremy Taylor.

tell how He approaches the soul; but by the life of Christ, by the power of His Spirit, by the beauty of the world, by the holiness of His saints, by the tenderness of friends, He does speak to the soul, and the soul speaks to God, and so rests."

CONTENTS.

Oh ! Thou Who deign'st to sympathize
With all our frail and fleshly ties,
Maker, yet Brother dear,
Forgive the too presumptuous thought,
If, calming wayward grief, I sought
To gaze on Thee too near.

A Son that never did amiss,
That never sham'd His Mother's kiss,
Nor cross'd her fondest prayer :
E'en from the tree He deign'd to bow
For her His agonized brow,
Her, His sole earthly care.

Alas ! when those we love are gone,
Of all sad thoughts, 'tis only one
Brings bitterness indeed ;
The thought what poor, cold, heartless aid
We lent to cheer them while they stayed ;
This makes the conscience bleed.

Lord, by Thy love, and by Thy power,
And by the sorrows of that hour,
 `Let me not weep too late ;
Help me in anguish meet and true
My thankless words and ways to rue,
 Now justly desolate.

By Thine own Mother's first caress,
Whom Thou with smiles so sweet didst bless,
 'Twas heaven on earth to see ;
Help me, though late, to love aright
Her who has glided from our sight,
 To rest (dear Saint) with Thee.

Thou knowest if her gentle glance
Look on us, as of old, to enhance
 Our evening calm so sweet :
But, Son of Mary, Thou art there ;
O, make us ('tis a mourner's prayer)
 For such dear visits meet.

JOHN KEBLE.

Feb. 5, 1872.

Ash=Wednesday.

THE TRIUMPHAL ENTRY INTO JERUSALEM.

*Go forth, O ye daughters of Zion, and behold king
Solomon with the crown wherewith his mother crowned
him in the day of his espousals, and in the day of the
gladness of his heart.*—CANT. iii. 11.

FOR it is written, "Rejoice greatly, O daughter of
Zion; shout, O daughter of Jerusalem: behold, thy
King cometh unto thee [a]." "Say ye to the daughter
of Zion, Behold, thy salvation cometh [b]." Called to
meet Him in the hour of His brief earthly triumph,
in a few days the daughters of Jerusalem must go
forth to behold Him wearing the thorny crown wherewith His mother, the nation from which He sprang,
crowned Him, in the day when He for ever espoused
His Bride to Himself. Then He bid them weep, for
themselves and for their children. But now He calls
to gladness, "not driving chariots, like the rest of the
kings, not demanding tributes, not thrusting men off,
and leading about guards, but displaying His great
meekness even hereby," even by the lowliness of His
one triumph here, the shadow and prefiguring on earth
of that triumphal entrance when the everlasting gates

[a] Zech. ix. 9.   [b] Isa. lxii. 11.

B

were opened to receive the King of Glory, crowned with the sign of victory.

Is not the lesson for us, for each one, at this time especially, to be ready equally to follow Him in gladness and in sorrow, remembering "that Baptism representeth unto us our profession, which is, to follow the example of our Saviour Christ, and to be made like unto Him?" The daughters of Jerusalem went forth to meet Him in His triumph, and that is not hard to do; or, at least, to seem to do; to thank Him and rejoice in Him during times of bright gladness. Only, perhaps, when we have thought we rejoiced in Him, it was really in earthly brightness, friends, comforts, mirth, and the voice of gladness. Did we at such times spread our garments in His path? for after the Apostles had brought the colt, they then gave up all; as St. Paul says, "I will very gladly spend, and be spent for you ᶜ." Or did we not rather try to gather up and enhance the brightness for ourselves, feeling secure in His gifts, and caring too little for others' needs?

He knows what best will fulfil that begun in us at Baptism, and "make us like Him:" if only we do not thwart Him, but try to say from the heart, "Surely in what place my lord the king shall be, whether in death or life, even there will also thy servant be ᵈ." For as on the Mount of Olives, lit up by the western sun, in joy and gladness, so on the way of the

----

ᶜ 2 Cor. xii. 16.   ᵈ 2 Sam. xv. 21.

Cross there followed Him a great company of people, and of women. If we go forth to meet Him, in joy or in sorrow, in the gladness of Christmas or the gloom of Lent, at the wedding-feast or in the funeral-train, it will still be blessing, still companionship with Him.

He calls us now, " sworn liegemen of the Cross and thorny crown," to arise from our beds of sloth, and come apart with Him for forty days into the desert; to put away some self-indulgence, to use some self-denial; to consider what sin is, and what it cost Him ; to consider what are our own especial sins, for which He died; that so seriousness may be added to our repentance, and strength to our faith. It is He, the Lord of love and joy, Who calls us, not now to feasting, but to fasting ; Who asks us to overcome our natural shrinking from what is hard or mournful ; Who bids us to sorrow with Him for a little while, that we may have fulness of gladness hereafter. The spirit in which we begin Lent is apt to colour the whole time ; either the spirit of grudging to part for a time with anything pleasant, or that which makes us rise up willingly at His word, following in the footsteps of all those blessed ones who long ago went forth to greet Him.

Thursday.

OUR LORD WEEPING OVER JERUSALEM.

*Mine eye runneth down with rivers of waters for
the destruction of the daughters of my people.—*
LAM. iii. 48.

BEHOLDING the city, He wept, wept for the slain
of the daughters of His people. The rejoicing multitude beheld only the fair city in the calm, bright
evening light of an Eastern spring, but He beheld
" the virgin daughter of His people broken with
a great breach, with a very grievous blow [e]." He, to
Whom time is not, beheld all the coming anguish,
"heard the sound of the trumpet, and the alarm of
war [f]." He "beheld, and, lo, the fruitful place was
a wilderness, and all the cities thereof were broken
down at the presence of the Lord, and by His fierce
anger [g]." He came now as the Healer and Deliverer,
and knew they would reject Him, and He wept:
" For My people is foolish, they have not known Me ;
they are sottish children, and they have none understanding : they are wise to do evil, but to do good
they have no knowledge. The whole city shall flee
for the noise of the horsemen and bowmen [h]." The
tears of Jesus! tears that men will turn from their
own true happiness and good ; not even the tears of

[e] Jer. xiv. 17.　　[f] Ibid. iv. 19.　　[g] Ibid. 26.　　[h] Ibid. 22, 29.

God incarnate availing, unless man will yield himself of free choice to God. Our awful liberty is this, that we may waste His sorrows for us, that we must choose good if we would have it.

To Jerusalem He said, "Thy way and thy doings have procured these things unto thee[1];" yet to her the full mystery of His love had not been made known; to her He had not yet come with dyed garments as one who had trodden the winepress alone. If, beholding the city He wept over her sin and punishment, does He not grieve beholding each heart once dedicated to Him, seeing all its blindness, unbelief, self-seeking, rejection of Him? Does Jesus grieve to behold my heart? grieve to behold all the future sorrow and anguish which it must endure as the due reward of sin, even if, through His infinite love, I am not cast out of the sight of His eyes? We know that He doth not afflict willingly; often, perhaps, He may long to bestow His comforts and blessings, temporal and spiritual, upon us; but sees that we are making it impossible, that neither in God's righteous retribution, nor in His mercy, can it be so. Does He weep over us, knowing the possibilities of even earthly brightness which lay in His plan for us, the joy and comfort which might be ours had we known the things which belonged to our peace? Even now, though it may be we must bear that our sins should take such hold on us that we are not able to

[1] Jer. iv. 18.

look up, still, as long as our probation lasts, we may turn to His endless pity, accepting the punishment, however bitter, of our iniquity; and remembering that the penances He lays on us do not prevent His forgiveness, our hearts may be so watered by His tears that they may not be wholly without fruit to Him for the time to come.

Friday.

THE CLEANSING OF THE TEMPLE.

Be thou instructed, O Jerusalem, lest My soul depart from thee.—JER. iii. 8.

OUR Lord came to the Temple on the day after His triumphant entry, to cleanse it by chastisement. He had uttered no word of reproof the day before. Yet He had looked round about upon all things:—

> " On Sunday eve with many a palm, .
> With many a chant divine,
> It came, that eye so still and calm
> Far searching aisle and shrine ;
> Happy the few, that hour
> Who with adoring hearts knelt to that gaze of power."

He, the "righteous Judge, strong and patient," beheld all the desecration, all the unrighteousness wrought in His Father's house, and was silent ; only the children's voices were heard, singing to Him as to God. "And for the Apostles also there was hence no small consolation. For that they might not be perplexed, how being unlearned they should be able to publish the Gospel ; the children anticipate them, and remove all their anxiety, teaching them that He would grant them utterance Who made even these to sing praise."

"But though He had done so many miracles before them [k]," yet the Scribes and chief priests believed not

[k] St. John xii. 37.

on Him. The children, the blind, the lame received
Him. Neither to the silent reproof of His presence,
nor to His open chastening, did the teachers of the
people bow.

He comes to us now in both ways; do we receive
Him like the children, or like the Scribes? He comes
to us in joy, with palms of gladness and the voice of
blessed children, bringing happiness to our homes;
silent and unseen, known only by His benefits and the
joy of many a day, but looking round about upon all
things, "watching by the Christian hearth," beholding the bodies once made temples of the Holy Ghost,
and knowing with a perfect knowledge whether they
are profaned by vain or selfish, or idle or angry
thoughts, words, and actions. Happy indeed the few
who in the silent blessing of His gaze forget Him
not, but watching and loving Him, offer themselves
a living sacrifice to Him. If His presence and the
children's songs of praise had sufficed to shame the
defilers of the Temple, there would have been no need
for the severe teaching of the next day. Yet happy
they also "who for His scourge made duteous way."
The last, bitterest offence, is to turn upon His chastening. When the Scribes heard what He had done,
they were sore displeased, they sought how they
might destroy Him, and they were angered by the
voice of the children. And this was the beginning
of their utter rejection of Him. So with us, with
me; Can there be anything so likely to destroy the life

of Christ in the soul as the angry receiving of His
chastisements? the turning from those who take them
meekly? As of old, so now, it is the childlike, the
poor, who take them best, bear them most sweetly;
but at least we may try not to be like the Scribes,
remembering that if He chastens those who bear no
fruit, or only evil fruit, yet the chastisement of our
peace was upon Him first; and that His Cross can
turn our heavy penance into a token of forgiving love.

> " Ah! my dear, angry Lord!
> Since Thou dost love,—yet strike;
> Cast down,—yet help afford;
> Sure, I will do the like.

> " I will complain,—yet praise;
> I will bewail,—approve;
> And, all my sour-sweet days,
> I will lament,—and love."

Saturday.

THE BARREN FIG-TREE.

*Wherefore, when I came, was there no man? when
I called, was there none to answer?*—Isa. l. 2.

OUR Lord's curse on the barren fig-tree is both
a parable and an alarming warning to us, lest we bear
leaves only and not fruit. " Who does not fear when
in this lesson he sees with the eyes of the heart the
withered tree,—withered at that word spoken to it,
'Let no fruit grow on thee henceforward for ever.'"
We know who were primarily typified by the fig-tree
found dried up, as now our Lord passed with His
Apostles to His last visit to the Temple, His last dis-
course to His countrymen. " For the vineyard of the
Lord of Hosts is the house of Israel, and the men of
Judah His pleasant plant : and He looked for judgment, but behold oppression; for righteousness, but
behold, a cry [1]." "Not that all were reprobate, for out
of it were called those who in sincerity and truth
waited for the salvation of God. For it was not in
vain that the Lord Himself had come to none but the
lost sheep of the house of Israel; and in others, after
He was crucified, and was exalted into heaven, He
found the fruit of repentance, and these He did not
make to wither, but cultivated them in His field, and

[1] Isa. v. 7.

watered them with His word. They lay hid here and there among thorns, as though wasted and dispersed by the wolves ; and because they lay hid among thorns, He did not come to find them, save when torn by the thorns of His Passion; yet come He did, He found, He redeemed them. They had slain, not Him so much as themselves. They were saved by Him Who was slain for them ; they were pricked in con- science, who had pricked Him with the spear; and being pricked, they sought for counsel; received it ; when it was given, repented; found grace, and be- lieving, drunk that Blood which in their fury they had shed. But they who would not receive Him were figured in that fig-tree. To this day we come to them, and find with them all the witness of the Prophets.

"But these are but leaves ; Christ is an hungred and He seeketh for fruit; but finds no fruit among them, because He finds not Himself among them. For he has no fruit who has not Christ. When He came to the tree seeking fruit, He knew that it was not the time for it; what the cultivator of the tree knew, did not its Creator know? but He sought fruit on it, and withered it away, as a parable in action; as though He would say to us, 'I have no delight in the withering away of this tree, I have not designed to do this with- out any cause for it, but only because I desired thereby to convey to you a lesson you might the more regard ; it is not on a tree without sense that I have inflicted punishment, but I have made thee fear, whosoever thou art, that dost consider the matter, that thou mightest not despise Christ when He is an hungred, that thou mightest love rather to be enriched with fruit, than to be overshadowed with leaves.'" To us He comes also, torn with the thorns of His Passion, has come since our childhood, not only as to the Jews before His death, but with all the sweetness and power of His ineffable suffering; His love no new thing to receive and believe in, but mingled with all our earliest and dearest memories. He comes, seeking some fruit besides the fair show of leaves, of outward profession. What has He found in me? what will He find now? during this Lent?

Monday.

THE PARABLES IN THE TEMPLE.

*The Lord hath rent the kingdom of Israel from thee
this day, and hath given it to a neighbour of thine,
that is better than thou.*—1 Sam. xv. 28.

Two distinctive points of teaching are common to
all our Lord's parables during His last visit to the
Temple. They set forth opportunities and privileges
accepted or rejected, and declare the righteous judgment of God in taking them away from those who
reject them, and giving them to others. The father
and his two sons,—the same command given to both,
—a free obedience needful; the vineyard let out to
husbandmen, who for a time might give or refuse the
fruit to the messengers of the lord of the vineyard;
the marriage feast,—the guests invited,—the choice of
acceptance or refusal in their own power. And in all
three parables there is the distinctest teaching of blessings rejected or despised being bestowed on others.
In the first, "Verily I say unto you, that the publicans
and harlots go into the kingdom of God before you [a]."

[a] St. Matt. xxi. 31.

In the parable of the vineyard, "He will let out His vineyard unto other husbandmen, which shall render Him the fruit in their season [b]." In the parable of the wedding-feast, the guests are called in from the highways to fill the place of the unworthy. The desire of our Lord for the acceptance by His creatures of His benefits is so great, that when those to whom they are first offered refuse them, the very stones cry out, those who were once hard and cold in unbelief, and so from the stones children are raised up to Abraham.

His last parables are a prophecy as well as teaching, a prophecy fulfilled before our eyes. The Church, His repenting son, formed of those once walking according to the course of this world, *has* gone to work in His vineyard; she has rendered Him of the fruit, in the lives of her saints,—the purity of her children,—the death of her martyrs; by the incense of her worship,—by her ceaseless intercessions,—by her works of mercy. His wedding has been furnished with guests. But as the Church was gathered in to fill the place of those who "judged themselves unworthy of everlasting life," so in the Church, there is the disobedient son, there are those who, partaking of all the blessings of His vineyard, will yield no fruit to the Lord or to His servants, there is the guest at His feast without the wedding garment. He beholds His Church as a whole, "a glorious Church, not having spot or wrinkle or any such

[b] St. Matt. xxi. 41.

thing, holy and without blemish ᶜ;" but each one of us must ask, "Am I, once made regenerate and His child by adoption and grace, daily renewed, daily forgiven and cleansed, so that I may have part with those who, having washed their robes and made them white, now walk with Him in white?" Alas! even to the forgiven, how many opportunities and privileges, once neglected or refused, are for ever lost!

> "Our faded crown, despised and flung aside,
> Shall on some brother's brow immortal bloom."

The crown of dutifulness which might have been ours, but which is for ever lost, as those to whom our duty is owed pass from our sight; the crown of love in word and deed to others; the crown of patience in suffering. "Whatsoever a man soweth, that shall he also reap ᵈ." Lord, let the harvest of suffering be in time, and not in eternity, through Thy forgiving love.

ᶜ Eph. v. 27.　　　　　ᵈ Gal. vi. 7.

Tuesday.

CHRIST'S ANSWERS TO HIS QUESTIONERS.

In vain have I smitten your children ; they received
no correction.—JER. ii. 30.

OUR Lord's manner of dealing with the three last
attempts to entangle Him in His talk is much to be
observed by us.   He, in Whom were all stores of
wisdom, Who *was* Wisdom, does not confound His
assailants by any new declarations of divine doctrine
or precept.   He deals differently with dishonest cavil-
lers and with earnest enquirers; does not teach the
former as He did His disciples, when they said to
Him, "Declare unto us this parable," but replies to
them rather after the manner of His answers to the
threefold attack of the Evil One in the wilderness;
making the very matter by which they hoped to entangle Him an occasion of clearing-up the difficulty ;
causing them to find the answer for themselves; in
two cases by appeals to that Scripture which they
knew so well, in the other by a lesson from one of the
homeliest things of every-day life, the coin in common
use.   To the questions of the Sadducees the answer is,
"Have ye not read that which was spoken unto you
by God?"   To that of the lawyer put forward by the
Pharisees, He replies again by words from the Book
of Moses.   May we not learn a lesson from this our

Lord's mode of dealing with such difficulties? There is One, very clever and crafty, who knows what an advantage he will gain over us if he can but disturb us, who always finds his best fishing in troubled waters. And the difficulties suggested by him, and which he often finds his best mode of hindering really earnest souls, are generally unreal, morbid, born of some desire to escape a duty, or to avoid seeing the plain teaching of God and of His Church. There *are* real difficulties and perplexities, times when we must come to Christ's ambassadors and say, " Declare unto me this parable ;" but a conscience kept sensitive through obedience to duty, will have an instinctive feeling of the difference between such difficulties and those which would only disturb the spiritual life; there is in the one case a certain quiet in the midst of doubt or difficulty, a " calm unrest," a contentment to wait patiently until an opportunity comes for finding the light : in the other case, there is a feeling of fretfulness, of impatience, of willingness to be disturbed, and to let our difficulty interfere with our devotions or our duty. How must we meet such times, which are in themselves a real temptation, even if the special difficulty suggested is unreal? How, but by trying to imitate Christ our Example, by saying to the Evil One, " Why temptest thou me, thou hypocrite?" and then casting about to try whether in the thousand parables of common life which surround us, in the (so-called) chance words we hear or read, there may not be a suffi-

cient answer to our perplexity; or whether, if those
fail us, we may not find it in some familiar words of
Holy Scripture. It seems as if it would certainly be
a surer and more wholesome victory over our enemies,
to baffle their devices by the use of such simple and
every-day means, than by extraordinary exertions or
searchings; the worst being that the very temper of
mind most likely to conceive or entertain such unreal
perplexities, is the one least likely to perceive their
true nature; but still prayer for help, and careful following of any gleam of light, will give us that reality
and simplicity which we might not naturally possess.

Wednesday.

THE WARNING AGAINST THE PHARISEES.

*Hell and destruction are before the Lord: how much
more then the hearts of the children of men?*—PROV.
xv. 11.

As at the end of our Lord's ministry St. John tells
us, as the reason of His rejection by the elders of the
people, that "they loved the praise of men more than
the praise of God [a]," so ·in this last warning against
their example, our Lord's teaching is directly against
the unreality, untruthfulness, and ignoble thoughts
which lay at the root of their would-be service for
God. As if He could be deceived by such service, as
if there were not more hope for those who made no
pretence of obeying Him than for these, in everything
bearing an outward show of religion. Yet has not His
Eye, resting in grief upon us, often seen that of us it
was true, that such and such things were done to be
seen of men? Unconsciously perhaps often; until we
watch, we do not know how hard it is to strip off all
such considerations, and to place the soul alone and
naked in His sight with Whom we have to do, asking
and receiving from Him the gift of the single eye, of
simplicity of aim. Yet nothing really noble or enduring has ever been done for Him or His Church, save

* St. John xii. 43.

by those who in His grace and strength had learned so
to feel; who, kindled with some spark of enthusiasm
for the Divine Person who once passed through life
desiring nothing but His Father's glory and our salvation, followed afar off in His footsteps, and were enabled
to behold with contempt that for which we naturally
strive. Therefore what our Lord says here against the
Scribes He says, "accusing them of vainglory, which
kind of thing was their ruin. This drew them off from
God, this caused them to strive before other spectators,
and ruined them. For whatever kind of spectators any
one may have, since it hath become his study to please
these, such also are the contests he exhibits. And he
that wrestles among the noble, such also are the con-
flicts he takes in hand, but he among the cold and
supine, himself also becomes more remiss." Our Lord
tries to kindle in His disciples, in those who in truth
were to wrestle unto death among the noblest, this
nobility of aim; by a few simple words, casting, as it
were, a clear intense light on the conduct which might
have misled them, teaching them what manner of conversation theirs was to be who were to sit in His seat,
as the Scribes in Moses' seat, and to be teachers and
fathers in His Church. All the grievous faults against
which He warns springing from the one root,—love of
men's praise rather than God's, the outward pretension
to holiness, the seeking high places, the desire to be
lords over God's heritage. So has it been ever since
in the kingdom of His Church, the kingdom of each

family, the kingdom of each soul. One of old writes, "It comes upon me even now to weep, when I hear of the first seats, and the greetings, and consider how many ills were hence engendered to the Churches of God." How many ills have been hence engendered to my own soul! that for which I should ever strive left out of sight, allowing my mind to dwell on the passing, worthless approbation or praise of men, until the thought of His praise and approval was dim and obscured. Those who live in kings' courts, and seek high places there, do not concern themselves as to what is thought of them among the lowest outcasts. Nay, rather, they who once love intensely are moved by no considerations which would injure their service to the beloved One. Our Lord, having warned them against this grievous pest of vainglory, instructs them how they may escape it; by humility. "He that is greatest among you shall be your servant: for whosoever shall exalt himself shall be abased, and he that shall humble himself shall be exalted'." He continually reminds them of this virtue. "On the Mount, beginning the Beatitudes, He began from hence." And in this place in His last teaching, He plucks up pride by the roots, shewing both the sins which it causes, and its consequence, "He that exalteth himself shall be abased."

f St. Matt. xxiii. 11, 12.

Thursday.

THE EIGHT WOES.

Behold, Thou desirest truth in the inward parts.
Ps. li. 6.

THE eight woes pronounced by Him Who came to
bring blessing, are directed against the consequences
of that vainglory against which He had just warned
His disciples. For this became a cause to them of all
their evils, namely, that they did all things for display.
Blinding others, they became blind themselves. Our
Lord rends away the false gloss and covering by which
they strove to disguise their sin ; by "one rough word"
shrivelling and burning up all such pretences, the long
prayers, the leading men away from the eternal truth
of God and fixing their attention on small observances,
the care for outward propriety, the vainglory which
shewed itself even in their condemnation of what was
wrong, when they said, "If we had been in the days
of our fathers, we would not have been partakers with
them in the blood of the Prophets !" O infinite woe and
sorrow, that He Who sees all as it is, should call them
whited sepulchres, hypocrites, serpents. David of old
used the same comparisons : "Their throat is an open
sepulchre, they flatter with their tongue," their "poison
is like the poison of a serpent ᵍ." Yet "that *they*

g Ps. v. 9; lviii. 4.

should be such persons is not *so* dreadful a thing
(although it be dreadful) as that *we*, that have been
counted worthy to become temples of God, should
become sepulchres, having as much ill savour. He in
whom Christ dwells, and the Holy Spirit hath worked,
and such great mysteries,—that he should be a sepulchre, what wretchedness is this! What mournings
and lamentations doth this call for, when the members
of Christ have become a tomb of uncleanness! Consider how thou wast born, of what things thou hast
been counted worthy, what manner of garment thou
hast received, how thou wast built a temple without
a breach! how fair! not adorned with gold, neither
with pearls, but with the Spirit, that is more precious
than these." Yet the gifts which we have wasted He
will give to us again, the garments which we have
defiled He will wash in His own blood, the temple we
have well-nigh ruined He will rebuild, if only we acknowledge our wretchedness, and try not to cover our
ruin with a fair-seeming show. "Men do any evil,
undergo any peril, to avoid shame. God brings before
us that deepest and eternal shame, 'the shame and
everlasting contempt,' in presence of Himself, and
angels, and devils, and the good, that we may avoid
shame by avoiding evil." Hypocrisy and pride, the
desire to seem fair to men, frustrate even His grace.
The utter folly as well as sin of such a desire is to be
considered. Even here it is not really successful, the
inward evil betraying itself; while with God's saints

the grace which they would rather hide than declare
oftentimes breaks through its earthly dwelling-place,
"casting a beam on the outward shape, the unpolluted
temple of the mind," making even the world acknowledge their beauty.   But were it otherwise, (and our
Lord speaks of those full of uncleanness who *appear*
beautiful outward,) the time is short.   Our bodies,
whether temples of the Holy Ghost or sepulchres of
all uncleanness, must return to dust; the countenance
which has deceived man will be hidden from sight, the
voice which has spoken untruthfully will be stilled,
and the soul, naked and alone, will be face to face
with Him, Who, all our lives, beholds us even as He
will do then; penitent, washed daily in the fountain
opened from His pierced side, or unconscious of our
need for cleansing, loving and seeking the praise of
men.   O awful moment, when even His redeemed must
feel how often they preferred that praise to His, when
in the utter loneliness of death they know that there
is none to whom they can fly *from* God, save *to* God,
the Father of our Lord Jesus Christ.

Friday.

THE WIDOW'S MITE.

The palace is not for man, but for the Lord God.
Who then is willing to consecrate his service this day
unto the Lord?—1 CHRON. xxix. 1, 5.

ONE commendation is uttered by our Lord during
His last visit to the Temple. He had looked round
about upon all things on the day of His triumphal
entry, had marked all there was to sadden Him, all
He must reprove,—the sellers of merchandise, the
money-changers, the Scribes and Pharisees sitting in
Moses' seat and corrupting the law of God,—and
now as He sits over against the treasury, His eyes
at length see that which He can praise. Only a poor
woman, but a present example of the contrary to that
which He has just reproved with such awful severity.
Poor, and a widow,—unlearned probably, since of the
poorest class; but taught of God, full of simplicity,
making no pretence, for she does not try to conceal
how small, (as men count,) her gift is, leaving it to
God to know that she has given all. The one bright
example to dwell upon and try to follow amongst the
evil against which our Lord warns us on that last day.
How shall I follow it? First, by giving like her, with
simplicity, be it much or little, remembering that it is
cast in unto the offerings of God, and that it matters

c

not at all what man thinks about it. Also, not to neglect to give through authorized channels, such as the
offertory, the clergy, societies sanctioned by the fathers
of the Church. She whom Christ commended did not
think, in her dutiful simplicity, that her offering was
too small to cast into the Temple treasury. Then we
must remember that what our Lord commends in her
gift is not its smallness, as seems often thought, but
its real largeness. Not until we have done like her,
and given all we possess for the service of the Church,
have we any right to speak of "our mite" as though what
is left for God, when we have freely spent on ourselves,
had any likeness to the gift of the royal-hearted widow.
And she, praised by Him Who sees not as man sees,
Who tries hearts and reins, had doubtless first given
herself to God before she gave Him all her substance.
There are two mites entrusted to the care of each of
us,—entrusted to me, which over and over again, at the
most solemn moments of our lives, in God's house, we
dedicate to Him, offering and presenting ourselves, our
souls and bodies, a reasonable, holy, and lively sacrifice
unto Him. He is present, hearing our vows, beholding our gifts, as truly as when He sat over against the
treasury in His Temple. But not only present then,
His Eye is on us in our homes, when we have left His
altars, watching how we keep our vows. Having
offered up body and soul to Him, do we, do I, remember that I am not my own, and not only sometimes but
always, glorify Him in body and spirit, which are His?

Do I try each moment to do that which I believe God
would have me do at that moment? or do I regard
only my own wishes and convenience? or let hours pass
in listless half-occupation or idleness? If I rest, is it
to gain strength for fresh service to Him? If I am in
society, am I watchful not to hurt others by example,
often speaking to God in my heart? Do I observe any
hints or rules given me by those in authority over me?
Am I watchful over that member of the body which is
a fire, a world of iniquity, and yet which may be so
especially used to His service? and over thoughts,
lest they should mar the sacrifice of my soul?

"Mystically, the rich men who cast their gifts into
the treasury signify the Jews puffed up with the
righteousness of the law; the poor widow, the simplicity of the Church, which is called poor because it
has either cast away the spirit of pride, or its sins, as
if they were worldly riches. She casts two mites into
the treasury, because in God's sight, in Whose keeping
are all the offerings of our works, she presents her
gifts, whether of love to God and her neighbour, or of
faith and prayer. And these excel all the works of
the proud Jews, for they of their abundance cast into
the offerings of God, in that they presume on their
righteousness, but the Church casts in all her living,
for everything that hath life she believes to be the
gift of God."

c 2

Saturday.

OUR LORD'S DEPARTURE FROM THE TEMPLE.

How is the faithful city become an harlot! it was
full of judgment; righteousness lodged in it; but
now murderers.—ISA. i. 21.

HE had come there now these three days seeking
fruit, and after that last mournful utterance of rejected love, "ye would not," He leaves His Father's
house "desolate," since His Presence was finally
withdrawn, and crossing the brook Kedron and the
narrow valley, He climbs the Mount of Olives, and
there sat down with His disciples, over against the
Temple.   Perhaps as He had said, "your house is left
unto you desolate," that His disciples, marvelling at
His words, came to Him, "shewing Him the beauty of
the Temple, and wondering if so much beauty was to
be destroyed, and materials so costly, and variety of
workmanship past utterance;" and He no longer talks
to them of desolation merely, but foretells an entire
destruction.   Most beautiful it was, and for thirty-
three years had been filled with a glory which the first
temple never knew, the Presence of God incarnate ;
yet now as He sits and gazes upon it, "comes wafted
from the Mount His stern farewell," leaving no blessing, but telling of coming judgment and anguish.

The awfulness of the lesson for us, for me, since He has "deigned the Christian's heart to call His Church and Shrine." He may have given many outward gifts to that shrine, many inward, beside gifts of grace,—He may have given beauty of body, natural beauty of mind, talent, intellect, genius, and men may speak of us as adorned with goodly stones and gifts, while in Christ's sight there may be nothing in us which will abide the day of His coming. For where He is not, there may be every other gift and beauty, and yet all is nothing.

"Christ, when He had foretold all that should come upon Jerusalem, went forth out of the Temple,—He, Who while He was in it, had upheld the Temple that it should not fall. And so each man, being the temple of God by reason of the Spirit of God dwelling in him, is himself the cause of his being deserted, that Christ should depart from him."

Jerusalem was lost, because she would not shelter herself under His wings. And this is what He requires of us, that we should accept the refuge which He has provided, accept Him as Saviour, Master, and Guide. "Doth He not justly turn away from us and punish us, when He is giving up Himself unto us for all things, and we are resisting Him? For whether thou art desirous to adorn thyself, 'Let it,' He saith, 'be with My ornaments;' or to arm thyself, 'with My arms;' or to clothe thyself, 'with My raiment;' or to feed thyself, 'at My Table;' or to journey, 'on My way;' or to inherit, 'My inheritance;' or to

enter into a country, 'the city of which I am Builder
and Maker ;' or to build a house, 'among My Tabernacles.   For I, so far from asking thee for a recompense of the things I give thee, do even make
Myself owe thee a recompense for this very thing, if
thou be willing to use all I have.'   What can be equal
to this munificence ?   'I am Father, I am Brother,
I am Bridegroom, I am dwelling-place, I am Food,
I am Raiment, I am Root, I am Foundation, all,
whatsoever thou willest, I am.'

" ' Be thou in need of nothing ; I will be even a Servant, for I came to minister, not to be ministered
unto; I am Friend, and Member, and Head, and
Brother, and Sister, and Mother; I am all; only
cling thou closely to Me.   I was poor for thee, and
a wanderer for thee, on the Cross for thee, in the
tomb for thee, above I intercede for thee to the
Father.   Thou art all things to Me,—brother, and
joint-heir, and friend, and member.'   What wouldest
thou more?   Why dost thou turn away from Him
who loveth thee ?"   Shall I, too, refuse to be gathered
under His wings?

Monday.

OUR LORD'S THREE LAST PARABLES.

*And he gave Joshua the son of Nun a charge, and said, Be strong and of a good courage; for thou shalt bring the children of Israel into the land which I sware unto them: and I will be with thee.—*DEUT. xxxi. 23.

Two lessons are common to these three parables,— one, that a time of probation, during the absence of their Master, must be passed through by all Christians. Only for two or three days longer was He to be with them, as He had been since they followed Him; and so in these last parables the thought of work for an *absent* Lord is especially dwelt upon,—the Lord delaying His coming, the Bridegroom tarrying, the man travelling into a far country; for man once more re-enters Paradise, yea, the Heaven of heavens, the land that is very far away. The other lesson common to all three parables,—that this probation and watch to do service to an absent Master most especially concerns those set to rule in His Church, and it is to

" His disciples privately," that these His last parables
are spoken,—to those who were to be the twelve
foundations of the new Jerusalem, whom He was
sending, even as His Father had sent Him, who were
to spend all, and suffer all, and to lay down life itself
for His Body's sake, the Church. To them He speaks
of the faithful and wise servant, made ruler over his
Lord's household ; of the virgins chosen to welcome the
Bridegroom; of the Master's own servants, to whom
He delivered His goods.   Leaving them now, He
warns them of their coming trial, but comforts them
by carrying on their thoughts to the time of His
return; tells them of the blessedness of the servant
whom He should find giving meat in due season to
His household ; of the marriage-feast prepared for
the faithful watchers ; of the loving welcome awaiting
those faithful over a few things. "What can be
equal to this honour? What manner of speech will
be able to set forth the dignity, the blessedness, when
the King of Heaven, He that possesseth all things,
bids us to enter into His joy?" What greater thing
can be given to a faithful servant, than to be with his
Lord and see his Lord's joy? For though these
parables are first spoken to the Apostles and their
successors, yet surely our blessed Master speaks to
me, to every one of us, by them. If we have not
been made rulers over Christ's household, yet "we
are stewards of our own possessions, not less than
he who dispenses the alms of the Church. As he has

not a right to squander the things given for the main-
tenance of the poor, even so neither may we squander
our own. We desire that what we give should be
carefully dispensed,—will not God require His own
of us with greater strictness, not suffering it to be
wasted at random? For if in worldly matters no man
lives for himself, but artizan, and soldier, and husband-
man, and merchant, all of them contribute to the
common good, much more ought we to do this in
things spiritual." He gave us the power to help one
another, that bringing us into need one of another,
He might make our love for one another more fervent.

All Christians have their own work to do, their
own ministry to fulfil in their Lord's absence; "and
every person, if he will but mark it, has a certain
sense and appetite for perfection, breathed, as it were,
naturally into his heart, so that he would rather do
a thing well than ill, if he could but do it without
trouble or self-denial. This is all God's silent teaching, to make us understand that whatever our ministry
is, He would have us make full proof of it." If we,
if I, try always to do it as to the Lord, present
though absent, I shall not then pride myself on partial
success. "The glory to come will quite drown the
faint brightness just at hand."

𝕿𝖚𝖊𝖘𝖉𝖆𝖞.

THE DAY OF PREPARATION.

The house that is to be builded for the Lord must be exceeding magnifical, of fame and of glory throughout all countries; I will therefore now make preparation for it.—1 CHRON. xxii. 5.

THE day beginning on Thursday evening, and ending on Friday evening, being called in all four Gospels the day of preparation—of preparation for the slaying of the Paschal Lamb, which we know was in the evening; (not on this Thursday evening, but on the following, when Christ our Passover died): a difficulty arises from three of the Evangelists speaking as if this Supper were the Passover, but the last as if it was not; for on Friday morning the Jews would not enter the judgment-hall, "that they might eat the Passover;" and St. John also mentions the supposition of the disciples' that Judas had been desired to buy what they needed against the Feast, which could not have been, if they were then themselves partaking of the Paschal Lamb. And St. Mark, though making mention of "eating the Passover" with an apparent application to the Supper, says expressly, it was the day "when they killed the Passover;" and St. Luke speaks of it as the day "in which the Passover must be killed." "For indeed

that day, from Thursday evening (at sunset) to Friday
evening, was the day of the preparation, and the Passover must indeed be killed on that day, as Christ was."
And the Passover must be eaten on the festival day,
the great Sabbath that ensued, which began at sunset
on Friday evening, the Passover being eaten at any
hour before midnight, not on the day in which it was
killed, so that we cannot consider the Thursday evening or Friday morning as the Feast. "Nor does it
seem likely that Judas would have left in the midst of
the Paschal Supper, nor would his leaving them have
been supposed to be for such a purpose, nor would
they have reclined at the Paschal Supper, for the Law
required them to stand." But though we cannot suppose it was strictly the Passover, since that could not
be eaten before the Lamb was slain, which we know
was on the Friday evening, perhaps we may consider
it "not as the Paschal Supper according to the Law,
strictly and properly speaking, nor altogether the same
by anticipation; but as the new Passover instituted of
Christ Himself, and having a reference to the great
Paschal Feast about to take place, it being the same
day then commencing on which the Lamb was slain,
though not when it was eaten, but "the day of preparation." Or as some suppose that our Lord did eat
the Passover by a kind of anticipation in some sense,
this Last Supper "partaking of the character of the
following Festival, particularly so when it was declared

that that Festival would not be kept at all (excepting
in the kingdom of God); so that this 'preparation'
was, as far as the Jewish rite was concerned, the consummation also." "But whatever that Supper may
have been as bearing on the legal Feast, we know that
it was the great and new Passover, the one Christian
Festival; and the very ambiguity in Holy Scripture
on the subject may have its lesson for us ; for as three
Evangelists seem to speak as if it were the Passover,
but the last as if it was not," so indeed it is the Christian Passover, the great memorial sacrifice, and again
it is not—it is not the Jewish Passover, nor the one
and only sacrifice on the Cross. And may there not
be this lesson to learn from the " day of preparation,"
—that it behoves us all, myself, to prepare for seasons
of especial grace. We know not, day by day, for what
we are preparing,—for what God is preparing us. We
are perhaps weaving, as we think, marriage garlands,
and they turn in our hands into funeral wreaths; but
this we know, that if we are careful to prepare to
receive Christ, we shall be rightly prepared for what
may come of joy or sorrow. Who knows what we may
miss of grace at Holy Communion, by not having made
any earnest endeavour to prepare a guest-chamber in
our hearts for Him ? Especially now may we take this
lesson home, for "the beginning of Lent is like a long
straight road, at the end of which appears the Cross of
our Saviour."

During Holy Week we shall be gathered round His Cross, but can we fulfil our duty of then giving ourselves up to contemplate it if we do not prepare for it? Can we do so all of a sudden? Who knows what we may miss of the fulness of our Easter blessing by not prizing or gathering up carefully the lessons of these "days of preparation?"

Wednesday.

OUR LORD WASHING THE DISCIPLES' FEET.

Thou shalt also make a laver of brass, and his foot also of brass, to wash withal : and thou shalt put it between the tabernacle of the congregation and the altar, and thou shalt put water therein. For Aaron and his sons shall wash their hands and their feet thereat.—EXOD. xxx. 18, 19.

THIS day seems, indeed, to have been the "day of preparation" in many ways; first, of preparation for that great Passover, when, in the sight of God and men, the Blood of the One Lamb, Who taketh away the sin of the world, should be sprinkled on the door-posts of His Church. But it seems also to have been a time of preparation to His disciples, fitting them for the great work which was to be theirs, leading them on from mystery to mystery,—the solemn supper, the cup given to be divided amongst themselves, with the words that it was the last they would share with Him on earth; then the washing of their feet, the Institution of the blessed Sacrament; His wonderful teaching, warnings, prayer for them. Now, when they had divided a cup of wine amongst them, and before the Institution of the Eucharist, He, Who had left His Father's bosom and unclothed Himself of His glory, rises from supper and lays aside His clothes. "The

Evangelist, being about to relate so great an instance of our Lord's humility, reminds us first of His lofty nature :—' Knowing that the Father had given all things into His hand,' i.e. the salvation of the believers, He therefore deemed it right to shew all things that pertained to their salvation, and give them a lesson of humility, by washing His disciples' feet." And as the High-Priest on the day of expiation was girt with a linen girdle, so He girds Himself with a towel, even as when having laid aside His Divine glory He, in the Virgin's womb, wrapped round Him as a girdle our nature; as He had said by His prophet, "As a girdle cleaveth unto the loins of a man, so have I caused to cleave unto Me the whole house of Israel and the whole house of Judah, saith the Lord, that they might be unto Me for a people [a]." And we are told that "righteousness shall be the girdle of His loins, and faithfulness the girdle of His reins [b]," that so by the perfect obedience of one Man many might be made righteous, our sinful bodies made clean by His Body. He pours water into a bason; not as Abraham and Joseph, commanding it to be fetched; but Himself doing it, He Who from His own side was soon to pour forth the stream which should cleanse the world. And then He stoops to the lowliest office of love, washing His servants' feet. "It is our feet, i.e. the affections of our mind, that are to be given up to Jesus to be washed, that our feet may be beautiful;

[a] Jer. xiii. 11.   [b] Isa. xi. 5.

especially if we emulate higher gifts, and wish to be
numbered with those who preach glad tidings." How
must they ever, through the long years of separation
from Him, have looked back to that hour, seen before
them that living lesson, the type of all that He was to
do for them and all His redeemed in all time, and the
practical teaching of humility and self-devotion for
others. It is this last lesson that our Lord dwells
upon in His words afterwards (for the mystical meaning was soon to be taught upon the Cross), when He
had taken His garments and sat down again ; even as
after His humiliation and suffering He took again His
human body, and ate and drank with His disciples.
His words then are spoken to me, to all. " Ye also
ought to wash one another's feet." "I have given
you an example, that ye should do as I have done to
you." Like the parable of the good Samaritan, "mystically containing all the economy of redemption, it is
given to us, to me, as a lesson of brotherly love, without which the high mysteries and doctrine contained
in it would not profit us." Do I try to take our
Lord's words as literally as possible? not only not
shrinking from, but eagerly embracing, opportunities
for serving His poor, not merely through others, and
by alms which cost me no self-denial, but "rising
from supper," laying aside my own ease and comfort
to do them good? A holy man has written, "The
very nature of such actions is now changed, for such
a practice is not usual among us as a servile office

at all, as it then was; and therefore this, if literally performed, would not be the same in spirit and character." But there are many offices as lowly, and sorely needed by Christ's poor, which we may perform for them, remembering what a saint of old tells us; "wherever this practice exists not among the saints, they do in heart what they do not by the hand, if they are of the number of those spoken of in the Hymn as 'O ye humble and holy men of heart.' But it is much better, and without controversy the true fulfilment, that it should be done by the hands also; nor let a Christian disdain to do what Christ hath done'," rather "wherever we see the print of His shoe in the earth, there may we covet to set our foot too." "And since with Thee is the fountain of life, and an immeasurable profundity of mercies, those whom Thou hast washed by Baptism, whom Thou hast bathed in Thy blood, whom Thou art always washing by forgiving daily, translate Thou from the pools and mud of this world into the most purified kingdom of Thy glory; where no unclean thing can enter; where there is no more need of washing; where our body shall be fashioned like unto the brightness of Thine own. According to Thy promises Thou must needs fulfil this in us, and Thou Who hast begun a good work in us, perfect and establish the same."

Thursday.

THE WARNINGS TO ST. PETER.

And Hazael said, But what, is thy servant a dog, that he should do this great thing?—2 KINGS viii. 13.

ALL through this awful night St. Peter is continually before us, sent with St. John to prepare the Passover, forbidding our Lord to wash his feet,— then eagerly claiming His cleansing,—earnestly anxious to know who the traitor should be,—questioning our Lord as to whither He was going,—warnèd by Him, —vehemently protesting his fidelity,—assured by name that his Master had prayed for him,—chosen to watch with Him,—reproached for sleeping,—defending Him with blows,—specially addressed and reproved,—following Him to the High-Priest's house,—denying Him,—meeting His look,—bitterly repenting. It has been thought that as he thrice denied our Lord, and afterwards was three times questioned by our Lord, three times professed his love, and three times received the pastoral commission, so that on this evening he was thrice warned, and thrice confidently asserted his fidelity; the first time being that related by St. John, when, after Judas had gone out, our Lord had spoken to the disciples with increased confidence and love, and that St. Peter asks Him, " whither goest Thou?" evidently from our Lord's answer, (more to his thoughts than to his words,) with the eager desire to accompany Him. The second warning, if indeed there were three, seems to have been that related by St. Luke ; the third, that which is told by St. Matthew and St. Mark, who both say expressly that it occurred after they had gone out to the Mount of Olives; and there is a difference in the circumstance introducing the warning in St. John and St. Luke; in the one, it is St. Peter's question, " whither goest Thou[c] ?" in the other, our Lord's words, " Simon, Simon, behold Satan hath desired to have you[d]." But whether the three accounts are of one occurrence or not, perhaps we may suppose that St. Peter's confidence was partly the re-action from anxious misgiving lest our Lord's words, " one of you shall betray Me," should concern him—that when his fears were relieved, they were followed by self-satisfaction and self-confidence; and this is full of warning for us, for me.

" Because the Lord said He had prayed for Peter's faith, Peter, conscious of present affection and fervent faith, but unconscious of his coming fall, does not believe he could fall from Christ." And how often in our spiritual life it happens that relief from some over-anxious doubts or fears is succeeded by too great easiness and want of effort and watching, especially if our trouble has been caused by any want of trust in God's mercy through Christ, and desire to be something

[c] St. John xiii. 36.   [d] St. Luke xxii. 31.

in ourselves in His sight. Then, if we are comforted
by those over us, there is the temptation to think,
"perhaps I am not so bad as I thought," which, if
yielded to, is certain to lead to carelessness and to
faults. Or if we dwell on others' sins, judging them
in thought or word, or thinking perhaps almost unconsciously "certainly I am free from this fault,"
how often we find ourselves falling into the same, or
the like sins.

One of old writes, "What mean these things, O
Peter? When He was saying, 'One of you shall
betray Me,' thou didst fear lest thou shouldst be the
traitor, and didst constrain the disciple to ask, although conscious to thyself of no such thing; but
now, when He is plainly crying out, and saying, 'All
shall be offended,' art thou gainsaying it? Therefore
He checked him, not compelling him to the denial,
God forbid! but leaving him destitute of His help,
and convicting human nature." And another lately
departed, "For this love, when it leaned on its own
strength, only led him to more signal feelings than
others: but hereafter he shall be much forgiven, and
loving much; and through repentance, he shall be
made 'perfect in love,' following unto death the
Master 'thrice denied, yet thrice beloved,' and
'strengthening his brethren,' sustaining the weaker
brethren, that they despair not of pardon, as his Lord
by His prayer had protected his faith."

"Moreover, observe how after the resurrection,

taught by his fall, he speaks to Christ more humbly, and does not any more resist His words. All this his fall wrought for him; for, before, he had attributed all to himself, when he ought rather to have said, 'I will not deny Thee if Thou succour me with Thine aid.' But afterwards he shews that everything is to be ascribed to God: 'Why look ye so earnestly upon us, as though by our own power and holiness we had made this man to walk *?'"

Oh! that our own unfaithfulness to Christ might work in us the same effect as in St. Peter! that we might resemble him not only by repentance, but also in the humility which the sense of his weakness wrought in him; that we might feel with him, " my sin is ever before me '," that so God may hide His face from our sins, and remember them no more.

* Acts iii. 12.   ' Ps. li. 3.

Friday.

JUDAS' TREACHERY REVEALED.

*Thy blood be upon thy head ; for thy mouth hath testi-
fied against thee, saying, I have slain the Lord's
anointed.*—2 SAM. i. 16.

IT would seem from the account in St. Matthew
and St. Mark, that all our Lord's words to Judas, and
his final departure, took place before the Eucharist ;
while, according to the order of circumstances in St.
Luke's Gospel, it would seem that it was after it.
But St. John, mentioning the eating out of the same
dish as our Lord, and the distinct declaration that
Judas was the traitor, (occurrences placed by both the
two first Evangelists before the Institution of the
Holy Eucharist,) says, "he immediately went out ;"
and St. Luke, being the only one of the Evangelists
who speaks of the first cup given,—"the Cup of
the Old Testament," as it has been called,—may, perhaps, have mentioned the Eucharistic Feast immediately after (out of the direct course of events,) "as
corresponding with, and the substitute for, those
shadows of the law which were then departing." He
also says distinctly that "*after* supper He took the
Cup," while the three other Evangelists all speak of
the detection of Judas as taking place *during* supper.
But whether he went out before or after the Eucharist,
we know that after the washing of the feet, when our

Lord had again sat down with His disciples, He says clearly that the traitor was amongst them; and from a discussion as to which of them should do this thing, the disciples seem to have glided into a strife as to their respective claims to being the greatest. And then (taking the accounts in St. Luke and St. John together), our Lord seems to have reproved them by a reference to His recent action: "Know ye what I have done unto you? Whether is greater, he that sitteth at meat, or he that serveth? but I am among you as He that serveth. Ye call Me Master and Lord, and ye say well, for so I am ."

He then leads their thoughts to the true greatness which was to be theirs. "You are right in supposing that you are on the point of being established in My spiritual kingdom over the world, in order to do good to mankind; but think not that from the benefits you shall confer on the world, you are to bring any credit or honour upon yourselves, for My kingdom is of a far different character. 'Ye shall not be so.' 'The servant is not greater than his Lord.' 'I appoint unto you a kingdom, *as My Father hath appointed unto Me* ,' a kingdom to be won through humiliation and lowliness." And having told them what their office should be, He adds words which it is of serious importance that we should remember: "He that receiveth whomsoever I send, receiveth Me." Do we, do I, really believe and act on this? Do I honour

 St. John xiii. 13—17.   St. Luke xxii. 26, 29.

Christ by honouring the office of those, even though
unworthy, who minister His Word and Sacraments by
His authority? or do I really honour, not Him, but
men, by despising and forsaking them unless I judge
them to be good? or if I do not go so far as this, by
want of respect to them in little things, and by for-
getting Whose commission they bear? St. Matthew
records almost the same words as used by our Lord
when He sent the Apostles with power and authority
to preach [1]. It was addressed to "the twelve," to
Judas as well as to the rest; for though evil, he
had still part of the ministry and Apostleship, was
still a herald of the King, and we have the words of
Him Who was Truth, that whosoever received this
messenger received Christ. But now He prefaces
the declaration, by saying, " I speak not of you all;"
for Judas' probation was over, he had forfeited his
ministry. Are not our Lord's words fulfilled among
other ways in this, that receiving His ministers as
coming from Him, we receive Him in the Sacraments
which they give to us? " When Jesus had thus said,
He was troubled in spirit," and again returns to the
loss of that disciple, whom at the last hour He would,
if it were possible, warn and save. He says openly that
one of them, one that eateth with Him, should betray
Him : He gives a token of who the traitor was to St.
Peter and St. John; and at last, to the question of
Judas replies, " Thou hast said." *He went out, and it*

[1] St. Matt. x. 40.

was night. " He went out, not only from the house, but from Jesus, in Whom there is light and no darkness at all." It was night without and tenfold night within; and the night without was but an emblem of that darkness which is without the Marriage Feast, when the door has been closed, and he that had not on the wedding-garment is cast out "into outer darkness."

Saturday.

INSTITUTION OF THE HOLY EUCHARIST.

Wisdom hath builded her house, she hath hewn out her seven pillars . . . She hath mingled her wine, she hath furnished her table . . . she crieth upon the highest places of the city, Come, eat of my bread, and drink of the wine which I have mingled.—PROV. ix. 1—5.

"HAVING finished the rites of the old Passover, He passes on to the new, which He desires the Church to celebrate in memory of His redemption, substituting for the flesh and blood of the lamb, the Sacrament of His own Flesh and Blood, and being made a Priest for ever after the order of Melchisedec. For if the heavenly word has been effectual in other matters, is it ineffectual in heavenly sacraments? Therefore of the bread is made the Body of Christ, and the wine is made Blood by the consecration of the heavenly word."

THE BREAD.

Three of the Evangelists, and St. Paul, who tells us that he received of the Lord Jesus that which He has delivered to us, relate the institution of this divine Feast. If we combine the first part of the four narratives, it is as follows:—"The Lord Jesus, the same night in which He was betrayed (St. Paul), as they were eating, Jesus (SS. Matt., Mark) took bread

(SS. Matt., Mark, Luke, Paul), and blessed it (SS. Matt., Mark), gave thanks (SS. Luke, Paul), and brake it (SS. Matt., Mark, Luke, Paul), and gave (SS. Matt., Mark, Luke) to them (SS. Mark, Luke), to the disciples (St. Matt.), and said, Take eat (SS. Matt., Mark, Paul), saying (St. Luke), This is My Body (SS. Matt., Mark, Luke, Paul), Which is given (St. Luke), broken (St. Paul), for you, This do in remembrance of Me (SS. Luke, Paul).

"It would seem as if there were two objects in our Blessed Lord's intention in His bodily appearances after the Resurrection; the one to shew that it was He Himself Who had arisen again; the other to indicate that it was the same Body, yet under different laws, being made Divine and glorified, and not subject to material restrictions: the one He shewed by the various visible manifestations, by eating and drinking with them, by allowing them, in unspeakable condescension, to touch and feel His sacred Body: the other was shewn by His sudden appearing and disappearing, by telling Mary Magdalene to touch Him not, by shewing Himself in another and unknown form to the disciples going to Emmaus, by His mode of vanishing from them, by appearing before the disciples when the doors were closed, and with something mysterious in His appearance that affrighted them, for they supposed they had seen a spirit.

"Would to God that we might ourselves profit by this instructive lesson of His gracious condescension, that

D 2

we to whom He has said, 'Lo, I am with you always,'
and 'This is My Body,' might believe it, indeed, to be
BHis ody; and yet might forego disputes on the nature of His Body and His most awful Presence, which
we must first span the heavens before we shall
understand;—nor let the Feast of peace and love be
made, by Satan intruding into that Holy Place, a
subject of strife and unjust judgments[k]."

"How shall we speak to Thee, O Lord;
Or how in silence lie?"

This is the hidden manna,—the Bread and Wine
given by the true Melchisedec to the true seed of
Abraham,—the cake in the strength of which Elijah
went forty days and forty nights,—the shew-bread set
alway before the Lord, taken from the children of Israel
by an everlasting covenant,—meat which came forth out
of the Lion of the tribe of Judah, dead, and behold He
is alive,—the cake of barley-bread overturning the tent
of the Midianite,—the Tree of Life in the midst of the
Garden, restored to us by the Second Adam, that we
may take of it and eat, and live for ever. Thou, O
Lord, Who never failest them that seek Thee, hast
found Bread wherewith to satisfy Thy people here in
this wilderness, and with corn and wine hast Thou
sustained them. Thou bringest us into Thy banquet-
ing-house. And we, what shall we say? how can we
even think of the Feast prepared? Shall we not say

[k] Rev. Isaac Williams.

to our souls in the words of a Father, "Consider with
what sort of honour thou wast honoured, of what sort
of Table thou art partaking. That which when Angels
behold, they tremble, and dare not so much as look
up at It, on account of the brightness that cometh
thence, with this we are fed, with this we are com-
mingled, and we are made one body and one flesh with
Christ. . . With each one of the faithful doth He
mingle Himself in the Mysteries, and whom He begat,
He nourishes by Himself. . . Let it be our one sorrow,
not to partake of this Food. . . Let no one approach it
with indifference, no one faint-hearted, but all with
burning hearts, all fervent, all aroused." Thou makest
Thyself known, O blessed Lord, in the breaking of
bread, taking away the fear of death, and the soul filled
with the love which is stronger than death can say in
peace, "my Beloved is mine, and I am His[1]." For
she is made one with Him to whom the Father hath
given to have life in Himself,—with the Bread of God
Which came down from heaven, and giveth life unto
the world. And if for our coldness and sin we feel
not Thy sensible Presence and sweetness, still we know
that Thy word endureth for ever in heaven, that coming
in faith and repentance, we shall not fail to receive Thy
Body and Blood. There is a difference in the words
used by two Evangelists after "This is My Body."
One says, "which is given;" another, "which is broken."
" Why is this? for of the Paschal Lamb it is expressly

> [1] Cant. ii. 16.

said, that 'a bone shall not be broken?' Why is this varied expression, but to indicate that it is His Body, and it is also Bread? His Body is not broken, but 'given' for us; the Bread is not given for us, but is broken.' "

But chiefly, in meditating upon, in receiving this Holy Sacrament, may we fix our eyes and thoughts on Thee, Jesus our Lord, avoiding all vain questionings, and seeking only to be nourished by Thee unto life eternal, Who makest a feast for Thy prodigal son, clothing him with the robe of Thy righteousness, putting the ring of the pledge of Thy covenant on his finger, and on his feet the preparation of the Gospel of Peace. Thy Name is great among the Gentiles, and in every place within Thy Church a pure offering is offered unto Thee, shewing forth Thy death till Thou comest, a Memorial before Thee, even as every Jewish sacrifice foreshadowed Thy one true and perfect Sacrifice.

THIRD WEEK IN LENT.

Monday.

THE CUP OF THE NEW TESTAMENT.

The Lord Himself is the portion of mine inheritance,
and of my cup.—Ps. xv. 5.

AFTER the same manner also (St. Paul). "Like-wise also (St. Luke), He took (SS. Matthew, Mark, Paul) the cup (SS. Matthew, Mark, Luke, Paul), and when He had given thanks, He gave it to them (SS. Matthew, Mark), saying, Drink ye all of it (St. Matthew); and they all drank of it (St. Mark). And He said unto them (St. Mark), This (SS. Matthew, Mark, Luke, Paul) cup is the New Testament in My Blood (SS. Luke, Paul), is My Blood of the New Testament (SS. Matthew, Mark), which is shed (SS. Matthew, Mark, Luke) for you (St. Luke), for many (SS. Matthew, Mark), for the remission of sins (St. Matthew); this do ye as oft as ye drink it in remembrance of Me (St. Paul).

"Thus did He give into their hands for His Church the greatest gift that He ever consigned unto the world, and with the same extreme simplicity with which in the beginning He created all things, by His word alone; imparting to them the laws and privileges which they were to observe unto the end. As at the first He said, 'to you it shall be for meat;' and as at last He shall say, 'inherit the kingdom prepared for you;' conveying thereby fulness of bliss and immortality: so now, 'He gave it unto them.' " He gave it to His Church, which He purchased with His own Blood, not only giving it as our ransom, but when " by His own Blood He entered in once into the holy place, having obtained eternal redemption for us [a]," He bids us drink of it, gives us this heavenly wine which maketh glad the heart of man. It is the Blood of the New Testament, for " where a testament is, there must also of necessity be the death of the testator [b]." And as when Moses sprinkled the people with blood to confirm the old covenant he said, " this is the Blood of the testament which God hath enjoined unto you [c];" so now, when old things were to pass away, the Mediator of the New Covenant says, "this is My Blood of the New Testament." Of the blood of atonement under the Law it was said, "thou shalt not eat of it," but of this, "drink ye all of it." St. Luke mentions two cups: of the one our Lord said, " take this and divide it among yourselves," "which we may say is a type of the Old Testament; but the other, after the breaking and giving of bread, He Himself imparts to His disciples, and He calls it 'the New Testament in

[a] Heb. ix. 13.   [b] Ibid. 16.   [c] Ibid. 20.

My Blood, which shall be shed for you,' signifying
that the New Testament has its beginning in His
Blood. The old Passover was ordained to remove
the slavery of Egypt; but the blood of the lamb to
protect the firstborn: the new Passover was ordained for the remission of sins; but the Blood of
Christ to preserve those who are dedicated to God.
For this Blood moulds in us a royal image, it suffers
not our nobleness of soul to waste away; moreover
it refreshes the soul, and inspires it with great virtue.
They that partake of it are built up with heavenly
virtues, and arrayed in the royal robes of Christ, yea,
rather clothed upon by the King Himself."

"We were hungry and athirst, yea, even nigh unto
death, and Thou hast given us to eat and to drink of
Thine own Body and Thine own Blood. Thou hast
called us, the halt, the blind, and the lame unto Thine
own heavenly Table; and hast bidden us to invite the
halt, the blind, the lame, to our own." Thou art the
true Vine, yielding the best wine for Thy beloved,
but, O divine Master, what fruit should they not yield
who are nourished with this wine! shall they not at
least be ready to bear the portion of Thy Cross which
Thou layest on them? Thou gavest thanks before
giving the cup, though it was the token of Thy bitter
suffering. And we, drinking of that cup, grudge to
shed one tear.

We may not speak aright of these divine mysteries;
even the Church, at the moment of consecration,

D 3

"taught, doubtless, by her Lord Himself and His Apostles, (so universal is the remarkable feature referred to,) so frames her memorial, by a change in her mode of expression, as to withdraw from the action, as far as may be, her own personality. Hitherto she has poured forth, with bold heart and lavish hand, all manner of direct address and service to God. But now she suddenly ceases from her own words. Struck with awe at a task so transcending all human speech, she stands reverently aside, and, for all sufficient memorial recites the words and imitates the action of the great High-Priest when giving Himself for the life of the world. It is His Voice, His Hand, that she summons to action now. In all Churches her own voice is silent, her own hand still. 'The Lord is in His holy temple, and all the earth keeps silence before Him.' In hushed and awful silence on her part, as of old, does the True Incense carry the True Sacrifice, and the Church herself therein, into the Holy of Holies. The great river of her Eucharistic praise and prayer, flowing in such mighty volume hitherto, is suddenly arrested, as Jordan of old 'rose up and stood upon an heap, while the ark of the Presence of the Lord, the Lord of all the earth, passed by.' Then, indeed, she resumes with fresh faith her work of service, 'the waters return and flow over all their banks, as they did before [d].'" And we, catching at most but faint glimpses of His marvellous works of grace, how can we speak of this greatest

[d] Archdeacon Freeman.

gift? In the kingdom of God, when, as on that last evening, the Lord of the faithful servants shall gird Himself, and make them to sit down to meat, perhaps we shall know what we only see in faint gleams on earth ; till then may we say with St. Ambrose, " I pray Thee, by that wonderful and unspeakable love, wherewith Thou deignest so to love us miserable sinners as to wash us from our sins in Thy Blood, teach me, Thine unworthy servant, by Thy Holy Spirit, to approach so great a mystery with such reverence and honour, devotion and fear, as I ought, and as is fitting. Make me, through Thy grace, always so to believe and understand, to conceive and firmly to hold, to think and to speak, of that exceeding mystery, as shall please Thee, and be good for my soul. Let Thy good Spirit enter my heart, and there be heard without utterance, and without the sound of words speak all truth. For Thy mysteries are exceeding deep, and covered with a sacred veil."

> " Honey in the lion's mouth,
> Emblem mystical, divine,
> How the sweet and strong combine ;
> Cloven rock for Israel's drouth ;
> Treasure-house of golden grain,
> By our Joseph laid in store,
> In his brethren's famine sore
> Freely to dispense again ;
> Dew on Gideon's snowy fleece ;
> Well from bitter changed to sweet ;
> Shewbread laid in order meet,
> Bread whose cost doth ne'er increase,

THIRD WEEK IN LENT.

Though no rain in April fall;
Horeb's manna, freely given,
Showered in white dew from heaven,
Marvellous, angelical;
Weightiest bunch of Canaan's vine;
Cake to strengthen and sustain
Through long days of desert pain;
Salem's monarch's bread and wine;—
Thou the antidote shall be
Of my sickness and my sin,
Consolation, medicine,
Life and Sacrament to me."

Tuesday.

THE PRAYER OF INTERCESSION.

Solomon had made a brasen scaffold, of five cubits long, and five cubits broad, and three cubits high, and had set it in the midst of the court : and upon it he stood, and kneeled down upon his knees before all the congregation of Israel, and spread forth his hands towards heaven.—2 CHRON. vi. 13.

HE to Whom the Father sware, saying, "Thou art a Priest for ever after the order of Melchisedec," Who had given to His people to eat of the flesh of the one Sacrifice which He was now offering, brings, as Priest, the incense of prayer. If the prayers of all saints are offered on the golden altar that is before the throne, and come up for a memorial before God, what must have been the sweet savour of this divinest prayer, the prayer of God the Son, the Son of Mary? We feel that the prayer of any saint is sacred, and shrink from intruding upon the intercourse of a soul with God. And though we are often told of our Lord's prayers while He was on earth, yet generally He withdrew Himself at such times, even from His nearest. But now, as in the garden later, we are permitted to be present at His prayer, to hear His words as Son of Man interceding for us. How can we ever read them, meditate upon them, remember

them, with sufficient depth of solemn reverence?
May there not be this lesson for us in our Lord's thus
admitting us to hear His prayer,—that we may carry
religious reserve too far? We cannot guard with
too sacred reverence our thoughts and feelings about
holy things; the more we do so, the more they will
be likely to gain in strength, and to be really useful
to others, as the violets and lilies which hide themselves give out the sweetest odours. But do we not
sometimes let this natural and right reserve turn into
a selfish and fastidious silence, when we might perhaps be a help or comfort to others? "There stood
no man with him, while Joseph made himself known
to his brethren * ;" but to them he opens his whole
heart, as now He, Whom Joseph prefigured, allows
His brethren to hear His most sacred words.

One not long departed has said, speaking to those
devoted to the care of the poor :—"I can conceive
nothing more sad than this, that when you are called
to minister to the poor, you should do so, indeed,
with all tenderness and lovingness, as regards their
bodily wants, but as to their souls, far otherwise :
that you should allow a feeling of shyness, or awkward-
ness, or reserve, to hinder you from speaking to them
of themselves, telling them of that dear Lord Who
bought them no less than you, pointing them out to
the only refuge, leading them—as far as you can—
to the foot of the Cross, teaching them, praying for

* Gen. xlv. 1.

them, praying with them. I know of no greater sin, with which Satan has any great chance of tempting you, than this. This is, indeed, to be a sealed fountain, but in a sense which your Lord never meant. Sealed, not for Him, and by Him, and to Him, but for yourselves, and by false shame. Think how it would be, if, hereafter, any one of your poor patients should accuse you at the judgment-seat of God, for not doing that which you might have done for their souls. 'I was able to hear, I would have listened : one word would have made an impression then,—as, never before nor since,—one prayer then might have found its way to the throne of God, as never again. But that word was not spoken,—that prayer was not breathed.' "

It is not difficult to know when words would be profitless, or worse ; and when we only refrain from them through self-pleasing and want of care to comfort or help our neighbour, for the religious instincts of the conscience will tell us whether we have acted in this matter with a view to God's glory, or not.

It will ever be impossible for us to enter into the height and depth of this prayer of intercession, yet may we not try to catch some faint notes of the harmony, and make them our own? learning from what He asked for us, His wishes for us, and trying to conform ourselves to them ; such as His petition for unity and love among His members. We know that He has prayed that those given to Him may be with Him where He is; how can we be fitted for that Presence but by trying here to follow His Will for us, and to *bear* His Will; remembering the path He trod, and that He did not forget to pray for us when so near to His bitter Passion? "Sweet and unearthly harmonies! Words from Him that loved not in word only, but in deed and in truth," in this hour of His last earthly parting and of approaching agony; of parting from those whom He loved as no man yet hath loved: words of melody from the Heaven of Heavens, strains to which we still listen, and as we listen, feel more and more that we understand them not, but love again and again to hear them! Words of Divine Love itself imparted to the world by the "Disciple of love."

Wednesday.

THE AGONY IN THE GARDEN.

Thou that dwellest in the gardens, the companions hearken to Thy voice: cause me to hear it.—CANT. viii. 13.

CAUSE us so to hear it, and with such awful reverence to watch with Him one hour, that we may gather something of what He would have us know of His Divine sorrows, and of what they should teach us. Once before the voice of the Lord God was heard, walking in the garden in the cool of the day, and man hid himself, fearing His words of condemnation; but now we may listen with trembling awe indeed, yet still with loving trust and thankfulness to the voice which tells us of the cup of trembling being taken away from us, the doom pronounced on the first Adam fully borne by the Second.

> " O loving wisdom of our God !
> When all was sin and shame
> A second Adam to the fight
> And to the rescue came.

> " O wisest love ! that flesh and blood
> Which did in Adam fail,
> Should strive afresh against the foe,
> Should strive and should prevail ;

> " And that a higher gift than grace
> Should flesh and blood refine,—
> God's Presence and His very Self,
> And Essence all-divine."

We cannot exhaust the lessons, the consolations to be drawn from this hour of unspeakable mystery and sorrow. In some ways it seems even more awful than the Cross, for then the struggle of mortal dread seemed passed, the Victim patiently suffering. But now we are permitted to witness that mysterious strife with agony, which all but crushed even Him, to know that "fearfulness and trembling came upon Him, and an horrible dread overwhelmed Him *." And as we turn from our own sorrows to dwell on His sorrows, we feel how gentle and light are ours, and yet that He knows all their anguish, that He once prayed the Cup might pass from Him, and that He would not hold it to our lips if He could spare it to us. We know that He, like us, longed and sought for human sympathy and comfort, and that it failed Him, that neither did He find any to comfort Him. We do not think enough of the added anguish it must have caused to a heart like His, when "coming to His disciples," casting Himself as it were upon them for help, they were helpless to comfort Him. For we cannot but think that even commonplace words, if lovingly spoken, (and what could be anything but commonplace to Him?) would have comforted Him then from those whom He had taken with Him, chosen to be His comforters. But this burden of disappointed affection and trust He also bore, and if among mere men the most highly gifted and finely organized have also the most

* Ps. lv. 5.

capacity for suffering, what must have been His power
of suffering? Whatever the most sensitive, tenderest,
purest heart can suffer, is but a faint shadow of what
His perfect nature felt. And all for us,—for me,—
for those who—

> "grudge one drop should fall,
> Out of their own dull veins for Him Who gave us all."

"For the hurt of the daughter of My people am I
hurt *." He overcame in that garden the powers of
evil, which in a garden had overcome the first man;
but must we not remember that even His atonement,
restoring us to more than the first Adam lost, does not
annul the temporal punishment of sin? The penance
pronounced on man and woman in Eden is not removed,
though "in dim figure mankind, who were exiled from
the garden, again return hither. Christ restores to us
that which we had lost, but sanctified by His gift and
blessed by His own adoption of the same. We have
lost our Paradise, our first and happy estate; we have
lost the childhood of our years; but in Christ we must
return to that Paradise we have lost, we must return
once more to lost childhood, and become again as little
children in Him. But this Paradise to which we return in Christ is not an Eden of delights, as it was to
the first Adam ; but a garden of suffering and expiation,
where we must watch and pray with the Second Adam."
To us it is still said, "in the sweat of thy face shalt thou
eat bread;" and He gathered no wheat into His garner

* Jer. viii. 21.

until He had poured forth His bloody Sweat. Our state is one of forgiveness, but also of penance; the sentence pronounced in the first garden must be borne. But those sufferings which in us could have no merit or satisfaction, He took part in and bore as the doom of man, making perfect satisfaction for us, and teaching us henceforth to bear them, not as a token of anger, but of forgiveness; of the love which, making us partakers of Christ's sufferings, would purify and prepare us to be with Him in bliss. "And even in this dark garden of sadness, Christ, in unspeakable condescension, seems to say it is not good for Him to be alone, but takes the Church to be the partner of His sorrows, saying, 'Come ye apart and watch with Me.'" To us the Church says the same words now, calls us to prepare to stand at the foot of His Cross by watching with Him through this season of repentance. If He came now, would He find us sleeping, allowing opportunities of grace to be for ever lost, as those who could not watch with Him one hour?

Thursday.

THE BLOODY SWEAT.

The yoke of My transgressions is bound by His hand :
they are wreathed, and come up upon My neck.—
LAM. i. 14.

HE, of Whom it was written, "He shall see of the
travail of His soul and be satisfied," wills only to gather
in his great harvest as man gathers in his earthly
harvest, in the sweat of His Face ; yet not as men, in
health and wholesome labour, but in an agony which
wrung His frame till it poured great drops of blood.
That precious blood which man on the next day
should shed, is forced from Him now by His mortal
anguish. May we not well pray, "By Thine unknown sufferings, good Lord, deliver us." Never on
earth shall we know what that anguish was. Whether
it were the weight of all the sins of the whole world
in all time which all-but overwhelmed Him,—of
mine, (O may I not add to their number,) or the
shrinking of His soul from the coming agony,—or
whether this were a special struggle with the Evil
One,—we know not. We know that just before He
said, "the prince of this world cometh and hath
nothing in Me b," that when in the beginning of His
ministry the enemy having measured his strength

b St. John xiv. 80.

with the King of glory, and having been utterly van-
quished, departed,—it was but for a season,—that
now an angel strengthened Him; the only other time
that we are told of this angelic ministry being after
that first temptation when vexed by the evil angel.
It also took place immediately after the Voice from
heaven had acknowledged Him as the well-beloved
Son; and during this holy week the same Voice had
again been heard, accepting His prayer.

Perhaps we may think with reverent awe that this
may have been the season for which the tempter
waited, and that besides all the burden of our sins,
and the knowledge of approaching sufferings, there
was now, at the end of His ministry, another awful
and mysterious combat with the adversary, so tremendous that He, the Captain of the Lord's Host,
the Man of war, "reels in that victorious fight."
But He conquers, and we in Him may conquer, even
though Satan choose the hour of our bodily weakness
and sorest mental anguish to tempt us,—even though
then when we most need help, it utterly fail us, and
that no visible angel comfort us; if only like Him,
being in an agony, we pray more earnestly, instead of,
as we are tempted to do, lying silent and crushed,
feeling as if even prayer must fail. Whatever our
agony, His as far exceeded it as the infinite exceeds
the finite. "He bore in its fulness the curse laid
on Adam, that in the sweat of his brow he should
till the ground, as on the following day He bore the

thorns it was to produce.. In both cases did the
Second Man bear the curse, not figuratively only, but
also literally; and that, too, in a fuller sense than any
other child of Adam. For those thorns it produced
actually pierced His bleeding temples; and the sweat
which He shed was no other than the blood of His
agonized heart, which fell upon the ground that had
been cursed for Adam's transgression." The earth
which shared in the curse of sin is watered by the
redeeming and renewing Blood, "for Jesus' sweat is
healing dew." Henceforth the corn and wine which
it shall produce are made heavenly Food for His
people. For "He That spared not His own Son, but
delivered Him up for us all, how shall He not with
Him also freely give us all things¹?"

It was written by a saint of old, "Many turn the
sorrows of the Saviour to an argument of inherent
weakness from the beginning, rather than taken upon
Him for the time. But I am so far from considering
it a thing to be excused, that I never more admire
His mercy and majesty; for He would have conferred
less upon me had He not taken upon Him my feelings.
For He took upon Him my sorrow, that upon me
He might bestow His joy. With confidence, therefore, I name His sadness, because I preach His Cross.
He must needs then have undergone affliction, that
He might conquer. For they have no praise of for-
titude whose wounds have produced stupor rather

¹ Rom. viii. 32.

than pain. He wished, therefore, to instruct us how
we should conquer death, and what is far greater, the
anguish of coming death. Thou smartedst then, O
Lord, not from Thy own but my wounds, for He was
wounded for our transgression. And perhaps He is
sad, because that after Adam's fall the passage by
which we must depart from this life was such that
death was necessary."

> " O generous love ! that He Who smote
>   In man for man the foe,
> The double agony in man
>   For man should undergo.
>
> " And in the garden secretly,
>   And on the Cross on high,
> Should teach His brethren, and inspire
>   To suffer and to die."

Friday.

THE ARREST.

*When the wicked, even mine enemies, and my foes, came
upon me to eat up my flesh, they stumbled and fell.—
Ps. xxvii. 2.*

YET this was their hour, and the power of darkness;
for though the spirits of darkness have no power at
all unless they can gain our co-operation, they had now
effected this; as, in like manner, the Chief Priests had
secured the help of one of Christ's disciples. There is
no word spoken by our Lord all through this scene of
treachery, in which we may not find food for continual
meditation: the first words, "Judas, betrayest thou the
Son of Man with a kiss?" thus shewing His Omniscience,
and yet not indignantly refusing the token, though
hypocritical, of affection, if even now this proof of His
mingled power and forbearance might move him to repentance. "O great manifestation of divine power,
great discipline of virtue! Both the design of the
traitor is detected, and yet forbearance is not withheld.
He shews Whom it is Judas betrays, by manifesting
things hidden; He declares Whom he delivers up,
by saying, ' the Son of Man,'—for the human flesh, not
the Divine nature, is seized. As if He said, ' For
thee did I undertake, O ungrateful man, that which

E

thou betrayest in hypocrisy.' " " See how up to the
very last hour He did all things for their amendment,
healing, prophesying, threatening."   Then, as the
armed band came forward, " Friend, wherefore art
thou come?" the last words to him who had been
His own familiar friend ; and then the calm advance,
as, when knowing all things that should come upon
Him, He yet stedfastly " set His face to go to Jerusalem." " So wonderfully do the two circumstances
seem to coincide and run parallel together throughout,
—that of our Lord's freely and spontaneously submit-
ting Himself to death, as the great High Priest Who
offered up Himself as a perfect sacrifice ; and that of
His enemies all taking a part in His death, and laying their hands, as it were, on the head of the victim."
He shewed that when He was weak, then was He
strong, by casting His enemies to the ground; not by
" one rough word," but by the simple avowal that He
was Jesus of Nazareth ; for " God was latent in that
flesh ; and the eternal day was so hidden by the members of that humanity, that it needed to be sought
with lanterns and torches, to be put to death by the
darkness! ' I am He,' saith He, and beats down the
ungodly. What shall He do when He comes to judge,
Who did thus when about to be judged? What shall
be His might when He comes to reign, Who had this
might when He was at the point to die? They in
their rage sought to put Him to death ; but He also
sought us by dying for us. And therefore, because

when they would hold Him, and could not, He shewed
His power, He let them hold Him now, that by means
of them, all unwitting, He may do His will." May we
not trace in this the rule of His moral dealings with
us, of how He would fain not leave us to our own
devices, of how He often casts us down when we are
bent on sin, though we, alas, too often arise, attributing
the hindrance to accident, and go on as though we had
received no check? He was bound, that we may be
free; He, with His fettered hands, binds the devil,
releases us from our sins, and gives us the liberty of
the children of God. If we will but stand fast in the
liberty wherewith He has made us free! but the same
powers of darkness which bound Him, are ever trying
to tempt us with false shadows of liberty; trying
to make us feel His easy yoke irksome; tempting us
with the seeming freedom of self-will, that we may be
tied and bound with the chains of our sins, having left
the service which is perfect freedom. But they who
enter "into the heart and love of the Lamb, find themselves so enthralled, so changed, so transformed, that
they verily feel the sweetness emanating from those
shackled hands." They desire to say with a saint who
refused earthly freedom, that he might preach Christ
to his fellow-captives, "O sacred Bonds, O shackled
Hands, take pity on this my liberty, bound and shut
in from all that relates to Thee. Would that I had
never given my heart to aught but Thee! It was not
enough for me to separate myself from Thee, and to

make myself the slave of my passions, but I have thanklessly tied and bound those holy Hands, wounding Thee more sorely than did those cruel cords. O Divine Hands, bound for me, imprison these eyes, that they behold not vanity ; take captive this wandering heart, that it fix not itself on the many follies which now fill it and separate it from Thee. In and with Thyself, O Divine Love, Thou bindest those who love Thee, Thou enchainest them, Thou winnest them, Thou keepest them fast ; they bear about, in earthly vessels, pure minds, transformed into Thee by Thy Presence and Thy Love. He that abideth in Thee, and is in bondage to Thee, what other freedom doth he desire ? Make me, at least, the prisoner of Thy Hope, therein alone to live, thereon to rest; that I may look only to Thee, follow only Thee, sigh for Thee, yield myself wholly to Thee, and on Thee alone repose,—my soul's life, my love, and my only Hope."

Saturday.

CHRIST BEFORE ANNAS AND CAIAPHAS.

The breath of our nostrils, the anointed of the Lord, was taken in their pits, of Whom we said, Under His shadow we shall live.—LAMENT. iv. 20.

BOUND by His enemies, and the desertion of His nearest causing the iron to enter into His soul, the Prince of peace is led through the streets of Jerusalem, beginning the weary going to and fro at the will of His captors, which must have so much added to His sufferings ; first, (re-crossing the brook Kedron, and entering Jerusalem,) to the house of Annas, thence sent bound to the palace of Caiaphas; then, after a night spent in enduring the mockery of the high-priest's servants, led before the council of the Sanhedrim,—from thence taken to Pilate's judgment-hall,—by him sent to Herod,—sent back by Herod to Pilate,—all this before the last weary journey, when " the very torturers paused to help Him on His way." We do not often consider these goings to and fro through the streets of Jerusalem as one of our Lord's sufferings, because they are, as it were, thrown into the shade by His greater agonies ; and yet how must they not have told in suffering on a frame worn with the agony and Bloody Sweat, with a night of unrest and buffetings ? Six such journeyings, at least, we are told of,—seven, if

the council of the Sanhedrim was not held in the house
of Caiaphas.

To Annas,—to Caiaphas,—to the Sanhedrim,—to
Pilate,—to Herod,—again to Pilate,—the seventh and
last journey to Calvary.   No alleviation, no comfort,
all through; He sees His friend only to hear him
deny Him with oaths and curses.   Surrounded by
those who were thirsting for His blood, He is content
to be dragged hither and thither at their will, expiating the many times that we go on our own way
with no thought of what He would have us do, seeking only our own pleasure, or it may be going on
sinful errands; taking these as all other sins upon
Him, as if they were His own, and saying, "the yoke
of My transgression is bound by His hand: they are
wreathed and come upon My neck; He hath made My
strength to fall; the Lord hath delivered Me into their
hands[k]."   "He hath hedged Me about that I cannot
get out; He hath made My chain heavy[l]."   "He
weakened My strength in the way[m]."   And we, if
like Him we are called on to tread weary paths,
count it strange.   We think if we walk for a little
time along painful roads that soon we must come to
pleasant paths.   But if, as so often is ordered for us,
one sorrow is but the beginning of many, may we not
gain patience from the thought of the repeated and
continual suffering of our Lord, no "hour of rest
before the grave," granted to Him?   And all for us;

[k] Lam. i. 14.   [l] Ibid. iii. 7.   [m] Ps. cii. 23.

for "although it ill became our Lord to be brought
before tribunals and councils, yet He willed to submit
to that affront and affliction, to the intent that His
doctrine and life might undergo the most rigorous
ordeal; and that it might be notorious to all mankind that He was, in all things, so holy, pure, and
perfect, that not even the utmost extent of that
malice, which seemed in these men to be indeed
hellish, could find a blemish in Him; and that we,
by means of His very adversaries, might be the more
confirmed in the truth."

FOURTH WEEK IN LENT.

Monday.

THE DENIALS OF ST. PETER.

Rejoice not against me, O mine enemy : when I fall,
I shall arise.—MICAH vii. 8.

THE accounts of the four Evangelists, taken together, seem to tell us that after his first denial, in answer to the maid who kept the door, St. Peter left his place by the fire and went out into the porch, perhaps to escape from the light, lest he should be recognised by others. It may, perhaps, have been while he was gone out, that another maid expressed her certainty that he was one of Christ's followers ; for while both SS. Matthew and Mark speak of " another maid[a]" before the second denial, St. Luke mentions that it was made to a man ; and St. John, that it was in answer to several, " they said therefore unto him [b]."

But neither of the first Evangelists say that the " other maid" addressed St. Peter, but that she 'began to say to them that stood by, This is one of them." When St. Peter returned, and again stood by

---

[a] St. Matt. xxvi. 71 ; St. Mark xiv. 69.   [b] St. John xviii. 25.

E 3

the fire, (as by comparing St. Mark's account and St.
John's, we see that he did before the second denial,)
it is, therefore, natural to suppose that one, a man
(St. Luke), and others with him (St. John), should
have charged him with what they had heard from
the maid. It has been remarked that this is the only
time where we are told of any woman taking part with
the enemies of our Lord, and no woman is mentioned
in the Gospels "as speaking against Him in His life,
or having a share in His death." Even a heathen
woman intercedes for His life with Pilate, while faithful
women surround Him with their love from His Incarnation to His Ascension, ministering to Him in
life, last at His grave, first at His resurrection.

After the second denial, it may be that St. Peter
withdrew himself again from the light of the fire, for
we are told that "after a while *came unto him* they that
stood by [c]," and this time it was his manner of speech
which betrayed him. SS. Matthew and Mark both
speak of those who made the charge in the plural
number ; St. Luke mentions " another confidently
affirming [d] ;" and St. John that a kinsman of Malchus
asked, "Did I not see thee in the garden with
Him [e] ?" The four accounts, taken together, describing
a scene where several join in asserting the same thing,
and individuals bring special circumstances in proof.

" Behold, that most firm pillar, touched but by one

---

[c] St. Matt. xxvi. 73.   [d] St. Luke xxii. 59.
[e] St. John xviii. 26.

breath of air, trembles all over. How many since then, how many, even boys and girls, have been able to confess Christ, and what an innumerable fellowship of holy martyrs, courageously and with violence, hath entered!the kingdom of heaven, which thing at that time he was not able to do, who received the keys of that kingdom."

If we think it almost incredible that one like St. Peter should have changed so utterly in so short a time from protestations of love and fidelity, truly felt, to denials of his Master, to oaths and cursing; may we not sadly remember that it is but too like our own ways, the difference in our frame of mind when at our prayers, communing with God, and through the day, if the temptation comes not to live as we have prayed? But though we may forget Christ, He does not forget us. "The Master hath not lost sight of His disciple;" but though a prisoner, and bound, "took great forethought for His disciple, raising Peter up when he was down, by His look, and launching him into a sea of tears;" perhaps permitting him to fall, "in order that he might be the less severe to sinners, from the remembrance of his own fall."

"It might not be that he on whom the Light of the world had looked should continue in the darkness of denial, wherefore, 'he went out and wept bitterly.' Blessed tears! O holy Apostle; the right hand of the Lord Jesus Christ was with thee to hold thee up before thou wast quite thrown down, and in the midst

of thy perilous fall, thou receivedst strength to stand.
The Rock quickly returned to its stability, recovering
to great fortitude, that he who in Christ's passion had
quailed, should endure his own subsequent suffering
with fearlessness and constancy."

Tuesday.

THE NIGHT IN CAIAPHAS' PALACE.

*O Lord, Thou hast seen my wrong: judge Thou my
cause. Behold their sitting down, and their rising up;
I am their musick.*—LAM. iii. 59, 63.

THE Lord, the Hope of Israel, was among them,—
in His own High-Priest's house, where He might have
looked for justice, for protection against the plots of
His enemies; but the gold had become dim; "the
precious sons of Zion, comparable to fine gold *,*" had
become "as earthen pitchers," affording no protection
to the innocent, broken in pieces themselves by their
own injustice. As in His temple, so now in the palace
of him who bore God's commission, He is rejected,
condemned, abused. His examination before Caiaphas
may have been a long one, for we are told that about
an hour intervened between the second and the third
denial of St. Peter; and St. John mingles the narrative
of the denials and examination, as though they were
passing at the same time; and the "*many* false witnesses," sought for, seems to imply some length of
time, as well as St. Mathew's expression, "At the last
came two false witnesses."

We may follow, in sorrowful and adoring love,
the whole scene as far as it has been told to us;

f Lam. iv. 2.

the first questioning of the High-Priest as to His
disciples and His doctrine;—our Lord's calm appeal
to His life, as when He said, "Which of you con-
vinceth Me of sin *?"—the blow given with reproach-
ful words,—the transcendent meekness of His reply,—
the many sought for to bear witness against that spot-
less life to which He had appealed,—many false witnesses coming,—their charges against Him utterly
breaking down,—two at least giving false testimony
both as to His exact words, and as to their meaning,—
our Lord's silence,—the High-Priest's evident surprise
as he arose and said to Him, "answerest Thou nothing?"
—Jesus still holding His peace,—His look on St. Peter,
—the High-Priest's adjuration, when, putting aside all
minor charges, he comes at once to the real matter, our
Lord's claim to be God of God, One with the Father,
—the silence of Jesus broken by this appeal in the
Name of the living God,—His acknowledgment of His
Deity, and prophecy of the day when His enemies
should be made His footstool,—the High-Priest with
rent robes declaring He had spoken blasphemy,—the
condemnation to death,—the buffetings and mockery
of the servants, to whom He seems to have been given
over till morning. This was the night spent by Him
in preparation for His sufferings on the next day;
everything teaching us,—both His silence, and His
words. Silent, when His own justification was concerned, "the silence of Christ expiating the defence

* St. John viii. 46.

or excuses of Adam;" "the silence of the eternal Word confounding the pride of the sons of Adam, who are always eager to justify themselves." He seems to say, "Thou shalt answer for Me, O Lord My God [b],"— keeps silence even from good words, but teaches us when we ought to speak, that is, when God's honour is concerned. He does not notice the many false charges concerning which it would have been useless to justify Himself, but at once acknowledges the one great charge which was true, though He knew that it would cause His death.

O perfectest and calmest courage! giving us the example that, putting the thought of consequences aside, we should constantly witness for Thy truth; comforting us with the hope that the very apparent overthrow of truth which such boldness may cause, shall be but the prelude to its final victory, even as the triumph of His enemies was the beginning of their destruction; since "the High-Priest, in rending His garments, acted a real and deep tragedy for himself, for he thus declared that the order of Levi, the Jewish priesthood, was rent, and even now no more."

"This rended garment stands in contrast with our Lord's imperishable robe," and also "in contrast with the rended veil of the Temple. For the Priest's garment was rent by his own hands: the veil of the Temple was rent by supernatural and Divine means, at our Lord's death, and the hearing of His dying

[b] Ps. xxxviii. 15, P.-B.V.

voice. For the opening of the sanctuary of God, the rending of the veil into the Holy of Holies, was the doing of God alone; no man had a share in this: man may rend and destroy; he cannot restore, nor open heaven." "The Evangelist recounts circumstantially all those particulars even which seem most disgraceful, hiding or extenuating nothing, but thinking it the highest glory that the Lord of the earth should endure such things for us. This let us read continually, let us imprint in our minds, and in these things let us boast."

Wednesday.

CHRIST BEFORE PILATE.

Then answered they and said before the king, That
Daniel, which is of the children of the captivity of
Judah, regardeth not thee, O king, nor the decree
that thou hast signed.—DAN. vi. 13.

WE are not told how long the council of the Sanhedrim, held when the morning had come, lasted,
we are only told that they bound Jesus and led Him
away to Pilate. The special sin which He had ever
tried to bring home to the conscience of the Scribes
and Pharisees was their hypocrisy, their regard for
formal outward observance, while neglecting truth and
justice; and now they give the greatest proof of the
truth of this charge, which seems most to have ex-
asperated them against Christ, for with "hands full
of blood [1]" they will not enter into the hall of the
uncircumcised, hoping to keep themselves pure to
eat the Passover. "They feared to be defiled by the
prætorium of an alien judge, and feared not to be
defiled by the blood of an innocent brother." They
revere the shadow, while seeking to destroy the reality.
If this self-deceit were only found amongst those
unconverted to Christ it would be less astonishing,

[1] Isa. l. 15.

but has it not been often the very root of the history
of the Christian Church in all ages? of individual
Christians, "something else substituted for the keeping of the heart?" Has it not been so with us? with
myself? we should, for instance, be shocked at omit-
ting the act of saying our prayers morning and evening,
or of behaving outwardly irreverently in church, and
yet how little do we think of inward irreverence by
wandering of heart. Is it not our temptation, who
outwardly adhere to religion, to fall into a way of
satisfying ourselves with formal actions, and so to
be often less alive to realities of goodness than those
who profess less? as we find that the Gentile judge
was the only one amongst those before whom Christ
was brought who tried to save Him, and acknowledged
His innocence. He takes Him apart, " suspecting
something great concerning Him, and wishing, without being troubled by the Jews, to learn all accu-
rately." The charge against Him is changed, it is
no longer that He claimed to be Son of God, but
that He said He Himself was Christ a King. It
seems strange that after our Lord had acknowledged
His kingly office, the Roman governor should, as
St. Luke tells us, have declared to the people, " I
find no fault in Him." But St. John fills up the
narrative, and tells us of Pilate's conversation with
Jesus, when he returned to the hall after hearing the
first accusation of the multitude outside; and that
after this conversation, (of which the three first Evan-

gelists only tell us the one question, "Art Thou the King of the Jews," and its answer), he went again to the people without, and said, as both St. Luke and St. John relate, "I find no fault in Him." For our Lord had deigned to address Himself to the little spark of good in the Gentile's heart, and he knew that the accusation, though it was one of all others which he would fear to refuse to entertain, was utterly frivolous. "He leadeth upwards Pilate, who was not a very wicked man, nor after their fashion, and desireth to shew that He is not a mere man, but God, and the Son of God. He undoeth that which Pilate for a while had feared, namely, the suspicion of seizing kingly power." Then we seem to hear the manifold and angry accusations of the priests and elders, "the more fierce" that they began to fear lest they should be baulked of their prey; our Lord's silence, Pilate's appeal to Him, "answerest Thou nothing?" and still that majestic silence; so that the governor marvelled greatly, having felt the power of His words, and not knowing that He Who would speak to save his soul will not speak so as to force him to release Him, but having convinced him of His innocence, leaves to him, as to each of us, the awful choice between good and evil. And to His followers in all times He furnishes example and comfort under the trial of seeing the wicked prevail; teaching them, when counsels opposite to Him are successful, to bear even that patiently, "understanding that God in this matter does not

require that particular service at their hands, which
they desired to offer, but another, very different, in
which He the more glories, which is silence and
patient endurance and humility. At such a time let
him leave his own honour to God's care, and not
concern himself about it, understanding that it is
His will that he should lose it; and let him leave
in God's hands His own divine honour, for He will
surely bring it forth victorious ; and let him only take
heed to imitate Him in all humility."

Thursday.

CHRIST REJECTED FOR BARABBAS.

Hath a nation changed their gods, which are yet no gods? but my people have changed their glory for that which doth not profit.—JER. ii. 11.

Is there not a lesson for us in the more than failure of all the devices which Pilate imagined with the hope of satisfying both his conscience and the people? the lesson that if we leave the straight path of right doing, the by-paths which we take, hoping without self-sacrifice or inconvenience to arrive at the right end, will not only entirely fail in this object, but will add to the evils which we hoped to escape. Pilate sent our Lord to Herod, thinking to shift the responsibility of the judgment on him; it did but add to the mockery and insults heaped on the Prisoner Whom he knew to be innocent: he was fain to use the custom of one being released at the feast, to save our Lord, and yet, as a concession to popular feeling, to treat Him as guilty,—the only result was that a murderer was preferred before Christ; he then tried to satisfy His enemies by inflicting a lesser punishment than death—it did not save Him from the cross, but added to it the extreme indignity and torture of the scourging. We may reject Christ openly, as the chief priests did;

or as truly reject Him, like Pilate, while seeming to
take His part, and knowing the good sufficiently to
desire to hide from ourselves what we are doing—
to put it down to necessity, overwhelming circumstances, &c. Yet any departure from the path of
right doing is a choosing of something before Christ,
with whatever excuses it may be covered, in order to
secure our own convenience, ease, pleasure, &c., or
even what may seem the good of others. We may
perhaps say to ourselves that our influence for good
will be lost if we speak the truth too plainly; that
by yielding much good we may save some, when we
are really giving place to cowardice, and rejecting
Him for the sake of something as unworthy to com-
pare with Him as Barabbas was. For nothing has
any worth or goodness except what flows from Him,
and that which is chosen instead of Him is utterly
worthless. What may seem to us great choices do
not often come in our lives, but when they do they
will be influenced by the little choices which we continually make. Should I not think every night whether
in some little thing I have not preferred my own will
or pleasure to what I knew to be right? I may not
have thought much of it, and probably Pilate did not
think it much that "suffered under Pontius Pilate"
should then be said of his Galilean prisoner; he did
not know Who He was, and, having tried many ways
to deliver Him, thought less of giving up a poor and
lowly, though innocent Jew, to His enemies, than of

giving occasion for a tumult, especially at the time of the Feast,—or possible insurrection,—for the accusation that he was not Cæsar's friend. "When the conscience is moved, and purposes of good are formed, it is the usual mode of God's moral Providence to allow temptations of self-interest or fear to occur, in order to try the sincerity of such resolutions." And if we fail in daily small trials, shall we not be likely in greater things to yield to popular outcry that which might have been saved for Christ and His Church,—which might have brought blessing to thousands unborn, even if we do not wholly part with Him and with His truth? It was so with Pilate now, yielding to the fear of an appeal to the Roman Emperor; but "the wicked shall fall by his own wickedness ͪ:" all ways of seeking for strength, and peace, and protection, excepting in God, are the ways that lead us furthest from them. This we see in our very moral nature, and in the very history of the soul of man, when it makes anything else its choice but God alone; it is not only punished thereby, but the very object which it wishes to avoid becomes its punishment. He who did not dare to be unpopular is everywhere spoken against, having missed the glory of standing alone for the right against strong temporary pressure; while the history of Christendom is radiant with examples of that courage made perfect through grace, that noble daring, without which

ͪ Prov. xi. 5.

nothing great was ever accomplished for the Church;
not in martyrs only, but in those also whose wisdom
was in their own day counted madness, although as
later ages. perceived, they spake but the words of
truth and soberness.

> " How sleep the brave, who sink to rest,
>   By all their country's wishes blest !
>   By ' angel ' hands their knell is rung ;
>   By forms unseen their dirge is sung ;
>   There Honour comes, a pilgrim pale
>   To bless the turf that wraps their clay ;"

may be as truly said of the soldiers of the cross as
of men who have faithfully fought under an earthly
banner. " The Lord is a man of war." Do we, do
I, think enough of the absolute need there is that
each of His soldiers should be brave? of the dread-
fulness and subtilty of the sin of cowardice? Do I
not shrink at times from avowing fully the belief
which might offend others? If we only dare to express truths which are accepted popularly, and bear
but faint witness—or none at all—to those which
happen at any time to be unpopular in some part of
the Church, should we have made any stand at all
for the way of Christ in the days when it was everywhere spoken against?

Friday.

THE SCOURGING.

The covering of it of purple.—CANT. iii. 10.
*This have we found: know now whether it be thy son's
coat or no.*—GEN. xxxvii. 32.

THE greatness of this special torture and shame
borne by our Lord for us, is noted by its being made
a distinct subject of prophecy: "I gave My back to
the smiters[1]." It is also one of the few out of those
"many things" which He should suffer, of which He
makes special mention in foretelling His Passion. On
three different occasions, St. Mark tells us that He
taught them how He must suffer many things; but the
last time, as they were going up to Jerusalem, He tells
them particulars of those coming sufferings; as though
He would try and save them from the sin of being
offended because of Him, by preparing them for the
indignities which they must see Him endure. He tells
them plainly that He should be betrayed to the chief
priests and scribes, condemned to death, delivered to
the Gentiles, mocked, scourged, spitted upon, killed.
We cannot but reverently think that those things
which He singled out from His unknown sufferings to
foretel, had a very special bitterness or agony. We
scarcely dare to contemplate or speak of this suffering,
for the depths of humiliation and anguish which it

[1] Isa. l. 6.

F

reveals are ineffable. Other circumstances are told
with detail by the Evangelists, but it almost seems as
if they were inspired with an awful dread in mentioning this infliction, which allows them only to tell the
simple fact.

St. Luke, who in recording the scourging of Paul
and Silas, says, "they laid many stripes upon them,"
does not tell us that our Lord was scourged, but only
of the compromise proposed by Pilate, "I will therefore chastise Him, and release Him." St. Matthew and
St. Mark only allude to it in the words "when they
had scourged Him." St. John fixes for us the time
when it took place; after the first interrogation by
Pilate, but before the condemnation to death. We
know, indeed [m], that it was a last unworthy attempt on
Pilate's part to escape from the pressure put upon him
to inflict death. He appeals to the people to release
Him,—first, as innocent, as found faultless both by
him and Herod,—then, as an act of grace at the Passover, and when Barabbas is chosen as the favoured one,
St. John tells us "*then* Pilate *therefore* took Jesus, and
scourged Him;" hoping doubtless, as his after appeals
shew, that "beholding the Man," "bruised for our
iniquities," they would consider Him already sufficiently punished. But to Him it only brought additional agony and shame, although it opens to us
a fresh fountain of His merits, and of strength which
we may make our own.

[m] See St. Luke xxiii. 16.

Only may we remember, when "shielded from any assault of the devil, that the covering is of purple indeed. It cost the King Whom we serve, the Lord Whom we love, all those purple drops which He shed forth in His agony in the garden, all those which He shed forth in His scourging, the purple that dyed His head from the crown of thorns, the purple from the five wounds—the five smooth stones wherewith the spiritual Goliath was slain. Our covering, but His agony; our shelter, but it cost Him His earthly life. This Rock could not give out its healing waters, unless it were smitten—this true Pelican could not feed its young ones save with its own blood."

He who willed that in a few years His faithful martyrs should have the agony and glory of deep sufferings for Him, would shrink from nothing which they might have to bear; and beholding Him, the weakest and most delicate found strength to endure utmost shame and the torture of stripes. "Ah me! God is stretched out before man! and He in Whom not one trace of sin can be discerned, suffers punishment as a malefactor. His sacred Body was all one wound for our sakes, because there is no part of our body but which ministers to sin." Now is fulfilled that which Thou spakest by Thy prophet, "there is no whole part in My Body *." No whole part in Thy Body, O my Saviour, Which alone of all the seed of Adam was perfectly pure; because in us, "from the sole of the foot even unto the

* Ps. xxxviii. 7, P.-B.V.

F 2

head there is no soundness[o]." How shall we, Thy members, indulge our body to the full, even in lawful things, far less, if by indulging it we sin against Thee? Shall we not pray especially at this time, that we who are chastened by abstinence, may also be gladdened by the same holy devotion, so that our carnal affections being subdued, we may the more easily rise to heavenly desires? For we are His Body—the Body which He would win to Himself, by giving His own Flesh to utter suffering. "Our sins are as scarlet," they are "red like crimson;" and scarlet and crimson is the robe which He wears, namely, our sins. He wears our sins, in order that we may wear His righteousness. He wears them red as crimson, but shall make them by His wearing white as snow; for He shall cast this aside, and His sacred Body shall be clothed with His own garment. For this garment is that with which He will clothe us, who are His Body; and His raiment is "shining and white as snow, so as no fuller on earth can white them[p]." For it is said of His redeemed, that they have washed their robes, and "made them white in the blood of the Lamb[q]." And His promise is,—"Though your sins be as scarlet, they shall be as white as snow; and though they be red like crimson, they shall be as wool[r]."

[o] Isa. i. 6. [p] St. Mark ix. 3. [q] Rev. vii. 14.
[r] Isa. i. 18.

Saturday.

THE MOCKERY OF THE GENTILE SOLDIERS.

All nations shall do Him service.—Ps. lxxii. 11.

THIS is His Coronation-day, crowned, though in mockery, by the Gentiles, whose kings should soon minister unto Him, bringing their silver and their gold with them. He had withdrawn Himself when the people would have made Him a King; now they had disowned Him as their King, and He accepts the crown of thorns which the Gentiles offer. He, the King of martyrs, first wears the crown which all His martyrs must in some sort wear before they receive the crown of gold; He wears the purple robe of martyrdom. There is no rest allowed to Him, no pause in His sufferings. "Then," when they had scourged Him, the soldiers take Him into the common hall, and gather unto Him the whole band of soldiers; then first were "the forces of the Gentiles *"" brought unto Him. For "the kingdom of heaven is like to a grain of mustard seed; which indeed is the least of all seeds ¹," and all the mysteries which were the beginning of the glories which shall fill heaven and earth were done in silence, in stillness, in apparent weak-

---

* Isa. lx. 11.   •   ¹ St. Matt. xiii. 31, 32.

ness. "Thus did the kingdom which was not of this world overcome the proud world, not with fierceness of fighting, but with lowliness of suffering : thus was that grain of wheat to be multiplied, sown in horrible disgrace, to sprout forth in marvellous glory." Yet "never in kingly robe, and imperial crown, and sovereign sceptre, were such glory, and such majesty, and such strength, as were in these." "His robe, and crown, and sceptre, are not weakness, as they appear, but strong in that strength which overcometh the world."

He, Who had given His whole Body to be smitten for the transgression of His people, now gives His sacred Head to be pierced with the thorny crown; He allows the soldiers to use His sceptre, the reed, to press it down upon His brows, while others smite Him with their hands. He, by Whom all things were made, and Who in the beginning had made the earth bring forth all good things, now, as man, bears the penalty, "thorns also and thistles shall it bring forth to Thee ᵘ." The second Adam reaps the fruit of that which the first Adam planted, yet, thus accepting the thorns which were all that He found in His vineyard, "His blessing on earth's primal bower" is renewed. He does not take away the penance given to Adam, and which all his children must bear; but bearing it Himself, He sanctifies it, and takes away its bitter-

---

ᵘ Gen. iii. 18.

ness, that we, "keeping stedfastly in our mind the King of the whole earth, and Lord of angels, bearing all these contumelies in silence, may imitate His example." The thorns of the earth having been bathed in His blood, are more precious than its flowers, and bear nobler fruit, if only with Him we will patiently bear our thorny crown. For He Who doth not afflict willingly knows that only pain can cure the wounds of sin, as His pain only can atone for that sin. As one of old has written, "Since the earth was polluted with blood; and thorns were springing up on all sides on account of the curse; and the devil having the handwriting against us, had us in his power, and tyrannized over us: on this account, the Lord, in spoiling him of all things, when He went forth to death, clothed Himself with these, to shew that His victory over death was for our salvation. He bore the blood in the scarlet robe; the thorns in the crown; the handwriting against us in the reed, wherewith the devil had written down that charge against us: in order that, together with death, He might abolish these things, and cleanse the creation from them: and instead of the thorns, might bestow on us the tree of life; instead of the crime of blood, might, by His own blood, wash the earth and us all, and instead of the curse might hereafter bless those that are on the earth, saying, 'Blessed are the meek, for they shall inherit the

earth ᵃ.' If sorrow follows upon sorrow, give us
patience, O Divine Lord of sorrows; let us never
feel as though it were enough, but remembering Thy
sorrows all through that night may we possess our
souls in patience."

ᵃ St. Matt. v. 5.

𝕸𝖔𝖓𝖉𝖆𝖞.

BEHOLD THE MAN.

I am the man that hath seen affliction by the rod of
His wrath.—LAM. iii. 1.

ST. JOHN only tells us of this last appeal of Pilate
to the mercy of the Jews. Both SS. Matthew and
Mark tell us that "when they had mocked" Jesus,
they put His own raiment on Him, and led Him out
to crucify Him; but St. John relates the intervening
circumstances while He still wore, though in mockery,
the scarlet and purple robes of royalty and of martyrdom. Perhaps we may think that as St. John had
followed Him into the High-Priest's palace, and as he
stood by the Cross, so he remained throughout the
Passion as near as he could to Him Whom he loved,
and that though he could not gain admittance into the
Gentile hall of judgment, yet that he was without
amongst the crowd, and beheld our Lord when He
was led forth by Pilate. "Then came Jesus forth,
wearing the crown of thorns, and the purple robe."
It is hard to read these words and not to think that

they are those of one who had looked upon that sight,
and who had received the image of his suffering Lord
with such vividness into his soul, that he is able in
these fewest words to convey to us the awful picture
of what he then beheld; and all the account of our
Lord's trial in St. John's Gospel gives us the impression of having been written by one who had watched
its various stages himself.   .

Now, after the scourging, the ill-treatment, the injustice, which Pilate had inflicted on Jesus, he yet
again testifies that He is perfectly innocent. "Behold the Man whom ye accuse of desiring to be a
King, behold Him, not bright with imperial glory, but
covered with reproach, in such utter abasement, contempt, and suffering, as may satisfy you, and know that
I find Him wholly guiltless, both of the charge brought
against Him, and of every other. I find no fault in
Him." He calls Jesus no longer "the King of the
Jews," but "the Man." "If upon the King ye look
with an evil eye, now spare Him because ye see Him
cast down. Behold the Form marred more than any
man's." But his appeal is in vain; the people, His own
nation and kindred, look indeed upon Him, the glory
of His people; they beheld the Star which had come
out of Jacob, the Sceptre which had arisen out of
Israel, but they then only looked upon Him to their
condemnation,—they beheld Him and found no beauty
in Him that they should desire Him. O awful lesson
for me, for all to whom in His Church He is now set

forth as Man and God, lest we behold Him with careless or unloving eyes, behold Him not as the penitent
thief but as the Jews did. For "here at length is the
divine idea of humanity; the one man, about whom if
we believe anything, we must believe that His life is
normal and regulative for the lives of all other men."

But our life and actions may as truly "cry out
against Him," as the voices of the chief priests and
officers. Pilate's answer seems as if he were struck
with horror and anger at their hardness of heart.
"Take ye Him and crucify Him;" but even then he
repeats his conviction of His innocence, "for I find
no fault in Him." The Jews seem, after this last declaration of Pilate, to have abandoned the accusation
first made to him against Jesus, that He said He was
Christ, a King; the charge most likely to be enter-
tained against Him by the representative of Cæsar, is
by him declared futile, and they return to the old
ground of complaint on which Caiaphas had condemned
Him,—that He made Himself the Son of God. All the
false witness, the vehement accusations fall away from
Him; and this only at the last can be said of Him,—
that "He ought to die because He made Himself the
Son of God *." He dies because He says the truth of
Himself,—dies, witnessing the same truth for which
His faithful martyrs suffered, that Christ the Son of
Mary, was also God. And the chief priests bore
testimony to the truth in spite of themselves, for

* St. John xix. 7.

"indeed according to their law, He needs must die : for the whole of their law is nothing else but a testimony to the Son of God, and that He needs must die."

Behold the man! fairer than the sons of men, yet Very Man,—the only Man in Whom God is perfectly satisfied,—the Man Who can of right plead for humanity,—Who, taking not on Him the nature of angels, but the seed of Abraham, — has perfectly fulfilled all for which man was created ; by His patience in suffering making satisfaction for our impatience and murmurings,—enduring all which was the reward of His well-doing, to make satisfaction for the sinful pleasures which we purchase by ill-doing,— by His "Lo I come to do Thy Will," making satisfaction for our wilfulness and disobedience. Beholding the Man, God sees at length One in Whom He is well-pleased,—One Who satisfies all His desire for our perfection. Behold the Man ! He has ascended up on high, claiming gifts for His brethren : "His right hand and His holy arm hath gotten Him the victory[b]." He has won the right to restore to humanity what it had forfeited, since He presents Himself a Perfect Man, the Flower of our race, to make satisfaction for the sins of men.

Let us, let me take the words of Pilate, and come into the presence of the Lord, and say, "Behold the Man!" "Look upon the Face of Thine Anointed[c]." Look not upon me, but upon Him on Whom Thou hast

            [b] Ps. xcviii. 1.   [c] Ibid. lxxxiv. 7.

laid mine iniquity. Behold Him, Man at thy right hand, ever offering for man the sufferings and death which He has commanded us to shew forth on earth, joining our commemoration with His, as we plead the sacrifice which He offers for us on high. Thou sayest to us, "This is My beloved Son, behold Him, receive Him, hear Him, love Him, imitate Him. In Him I give thee all My treasures, a remedy for all thy wants, deliverance in all thy afflictions, satisfaction for all that thou owest to Me, the Mediator of all thy prayers, a treasury of every good thou canst desire."

"Beholding Him, we may be transformed into His image and likeness; worshipping Him, we may be delivered from every false worship; believing on Him, we may receive power to become all which sons of God, that name which we have borne from our baptisms, involves."

Tuesday.

THE CONDEMNATION TO DEATH.

Mine heritage is unto Me as a lion in the forest ; it crieth out against Me.—JER. xii. 8.

HE of Whom it is written, "God shall come, and shall not keep silence [d]," is now, as "a man that heareth not [e]." We are told that He was silent before the Chief Priest,—before the Jewish Council,—before Herod; and once, earlier in the trial before Pilate, it is written by St. Matthew, that "He answered him to never a word [f]." Now, for the fifth time, we read of the awful silence of Jesus,—"when He answered not, silent as the sheep; when He answered, teaching as the Shepherd." Pilate was the more afraid, when he hears that his prisoner claims to be Son of God. He doubtless feared before, felt that He Who stood before him was not as other men, and now he asks Him, "Whence art Thou?" More than a year before, at the Feast of Tabernacles, the Jews had said, "When Christ cometh, no man knoweth whence He is [g];" and He, not as now, silent, had cried in the temple, "Ye both know Me, and ye know whence I am : He that sent Me is true, Whom ye

[d] Ps. l. 3.   [e] Ibid. xxxviii. 14.   [f] St. Matt. xxvii. 14.
[g] St. John vii. 27.

know not [h]." "That is to say, 'Ye both know Me, and know Me not; ye both know Me, and whence I am ye know,'—in regard of the flesh and shape of man which He bore, but not in respect of the Godhead.—'And I am not come of Myself, but He that sent Me is true, Whom ye know not;' howbeit, 'that ye may know Him, believe on Him Whom He sent, and ye will know [i].'"

It was concerning His Godhead that Pilate enquired, but no man "knoweth the Father save the Son, and he to whomsoever the Son will reveal Him [k]," and the time was past when He had graciously answered Pilate, and tried to lead him to the truth. "For he ought to have resisted, and rescued Him, instead of which He had yielded to the fury of the Jews. Wherefore seeing that he asked questions without object, He answers him no more." He answers not, and when Pilate speaks to Him sternly as one having authority, He opens His lips for the last time to remind him whence that authority comes, and of the sin for which he will have to give account. "From thenceforth Pilate sought to release Him," (i.e. to this intent, that he might not have sin by putting to death an innocent man); Him to Whom he had preferred Barabbas, Whom he had scourged, given over to the mockery of the soldiers, led forth crowned and bleeding. The Jews again shift their ground of complaint, perceiving that our Lord's claim to

[h] St. John vii. 28. [i] Ibid. viii. 19. [k] St. Matt. xi. 27.

Divinity does not weigh against Him with the Roman
Governor, but rather increases his awe of the prisoner.
"Pilate was afraid, not of violating their law by spar-
ing Him, but of killing the Son of God, in killing
Him." They return to the charge which they knew
he would most fear to dismiss as groundless, since
"whosoever maketh himself a king, speaketh against
Cæsar," and "he could not treat his master Cæsar
with the same contempt with which he treated the
law of a foreign nation." Yet not immediately did
Pilate yield to the threat, "if thou let this man go,
thou art not Cæsar's friend;" our Lord's words during
his first interrogation seem to have convinced him
fully that His kingdom was indeed not of this world,
and he tries once more to persuade the Jews to save
Him. He had been taken back into the judgment-
hall, and now Pilate brings Him forth again, removes
also from the inner to an outer tribunal, and again
presents Jesus to His nation, saying, "Behold your
King." Perhaps it was when he was set down on
this judgment-seat that he received the last warning
in the message from his wife which might have saved
him; it may have influenced him for the moment to
disregard the threat of disloyalty, and present our
Lord as the King Whom they should serve, even
answering the cry of "Away with Him, crucify Him,"
by the question, "Shall I crucify your King?" But
now the nation and Church to which our Lord had
come, finally reject Him by the words of their chief

rulers, "We have no king but Cæsar." "They would not receive the Prince of Peace, riding on an ass in His gentle coming; when the babes sang of His Advent in the Temple, and the Prophet bade them rejoice, saying, 'Rejoice greatly, thou daughter of Sion, behold, thy King cometh.' Therefore in great mourning they shall receive their own chosen Cæsar, coming with his army and unparalleled destruction." As Moses had forewarned them that if they would not serve God with "joyfulness and with gladness of heart," they should "serve their enemies which the Lord should send against them, in hunger, and in thirst, and in nakedness, and in want of all things: that He should put a yoke of iron upon their neck, until He had destroyed them[1]." They have their way at last; Pilate yields; "then delivered he Him therefore unto them to be crucified," though still to the last witnessing to His innocence, washing his hands before them, declaring himself free from the Blood of the just Person; perhaps thus even to the very last trying to reconcile his duty with his fears, hoping thus to satisfy the charge of his wife, "have thou nothing to do with that just Man." "The judge, then, who is thus compelled to give sentence against the Lord, does not convict the accused, but the accusers, pronouncing innocent Him Who is to be crucified." And then the "whole people join with their chief priests, and accept the guilt of His Blood for themselves and for their

[1] Deut. xxviii. 48, 49.

children." They were about to mark their door-posts with the blood of the typical lamb, but the Blood of the true Paschal Lamb they seek, not for cleansing, but for condemnation. Are there many things for which we ought more to pray than that we may not be left to have our own way? for which we ought more to thank God than that He has not granted us our own choice? "What shall I say, O Lord, when I see Thee, for my sake, delivered up to the perverse will of Thine enemies, and yet hold back from committing myself, without reserve, to Thy most holy will?"

𝕲𝖊𝖉𝖓𝖊𝖘𝖉𝖆𝖞.

THE WAY OF THE CROSS.

And Abraham took the wood of the burnt offering, and laid it upon Isaac his son; and he took the fire in his hand, and a knife; and they went both of them together.—GEN. xxii. 6.

THE last and most solemn days of Lent are near; shall we not try, by following our Lord along His Way of Sorrows, to prepare ourselves for standing by His Cross, learning something more each year of what that Cross is to us and for us? All the Evangelists use the same expression in relating what followed after Pilate had delivered Jesus to the will of His enemies, "they led Him away;" as it was written, "He is brought as a lamb to the slaughter ᵐ." Both these sentences convey the impression of our Lord being bound and led captive by chains or cords. " O the Hope of Israel, the Saviour thereof in time of trouble, why shouldest Thou be as a man astonied, as a mighty man that cannot save ⁿ?" His Feet trod that path of pain because our feet have been swift to tread paths of sin; He was led captive at the will of His enemies because we have followed our own self-willed choice, not walking in His ways and taking His easy yoke and light burden on us, but seeking our own

ᵐ Isa. liii. 7.   ⁿ Jer. xiv. 8, 9.

pleasure and profit, even when we knew it would involve some neglect of what was most for His glory.

They took off from Him the purple robes, putting on Him His own seamless raiment, and then, as Abraham had laid the wood of the burnt-offering on Isaac, they lay upon His shoulders the wood of the Cross. "As a victim of God, He carries the wood for His sacrifice; as a Conqueror, the arms with which He is to conquer the world; as a King, the sceptre with which He is to rule His people." For it had been written of Him, "the government shall be on His shoulder [o]," and "the key of the house of David will I lay upon His shoulder [p]." He bears it, as the Levite bore the ark on his shoulders, "for this Cross is the ark of our salvation." "Christ therefore bearing His Cross, already as a conqueror, carried His trophies. The Cross is laid upon His shoulders, because, whether Simon or Himself bore it, both Christ bore it in the man, and the man in Christ." "For of that candle which was to be lighted and not to be put under a bushel, the Lord bore the candlestick." And bearing it, He would still teach us. Holy Scripture tells us of two incidents on that mournful journey, —the meeting with Simon of Cyrene, and His words to the daughters of Jerusalem. St. John tells us that He went forth "bearing His Cross;" the other three Evangelists all relate that it was laid upon the Cyrenian. Our Lord must have borne it part of the

[o] Isa. ix. 6. [p] Ibid. xxii. 22.

way, for we are told that it was "as they came out,"
perhaps at the gate of the city, that they met Simon,
coming out of the country. We cannot think, from
the rest of the narrative, that anything but His utter
inability to bear it any farther would have moved His
enemies to give Him even this relief. But now His
disciples see in mysterious living parable the lesson
which He had often tried to teach them, that whosoever would be His disciple, must take up his cross
and follow Him. And the enthusiasm which He
kindled in His followers, the "awful charm" "cast
o'er hope and memory, o'er life and death" by His
Cross, had surely its root in this, that whatsoever He
taught in word, He taught far more in action. "I
have given you an example [q]." Only He could say
that He had done so with perfectness, but it is the
source of all influence for good along His dazzling
way, among those of earth's gems, who catching His
fire have shone as lights in the world. To *be* good more
than to do good has been the best teaching, or rather
to be good *will* do most good. So in action, "strong
when He is weak," He "sets forth this mystery, that
He Himself first of all lifts the Cross on Himself, and
then delivers it to His members to lift. It is not
a Jew who bears the Cross, but a stranger and a
foreigner." We think of the blessedness of Simon
thus allowed to bear the Cross after Jesus, "filling
up that which is behind of the sufferings of Christ [r];"

[q] St. John xiii. 15.   [r] Col. I. 24.

and yet how often we—each of us, I—shrink from that
very privilege, think to approach Him without bearing
any slight share of His Cross !

The only words of our Lord recorded during this
Way of Sorrows are told us by St. Luke, the pitiful
physician. There followed Him a great company of
people, and of women; and it is to the latter, be-
wailing and lamenting Him, that He turns and speaks.
It is not enough that He should with perfectness *bear*,
but even now, faint and bruised and bleeding, He
takes thought for others.   He teaches us, when sorrow
comes to us, not to let it engross us, not to think it
sufficient to try and bear our own cross, but even then
to think of others, to do what we can to lighten
their sorrows.   And surely " we cannot but reverently
adore the exceeding carefulness of our Lord even now
in watching for every occasion of doing good : and
the admonition we cannot but consider as intended
for us all; that when we feel our human sympathies
and compassions moved towards Him at the recital
of His sufferings, we are to think that He turns to
us, and tells us to think of ourselves, and of our own
sins, that occasioned those sufferings ; that when
we venture to approach and gaze on Him, by these
contemplations, we forget not ourselves also."   But
blessed are they who leave their " common daily path "
to mourn for Christ's sufferings, for they will hear
His Voice speaking to and teaching them.

Thursday.

THE CRUCIFIXION.

King Solomon made Himself a bed of the wood of Lebanon.—CANT. iii. 9 (marg. reading).

THE Way of Sorrows is past, the most august and mournful procession that this earth ever saw is closed, and He Who made the glory of that procession, as He is the glory of heaven and earth, is lifted up between heaven and earth, finding no resting-place amidst all that He had created, except on that Tree which should become to us the Tree of Life, planted in the midst of the Garden of His Church.

"That Tree, of which the Bride in the Canticles makes mention, 'I said, I will go up to the Palm-tree, I will take hold of the boughs thereof[a].' A true Palm-tree, growing in the dry and parched deserts of this world, in a thirsty land where no water is[b]; for the dry and sapless wood once set on Mount Calvary, has now 'blossomed abundantly,' and its branches are the branches of honour and immortality, meet for those that overcome, and sit down at the everlasting marriage-supper."

It was the third hour, and they crucified Him; nine o'clock according to our time, the time of the morning

---

[a] Cant. vii. 8. [b] Ps. lxiii. 1.

sacrifice, when He ascended the Altar of the Cross,
"spreading out His hands all the day unto a rebel-
lious people ;" "encompassing the world in His out-
stretched arms, and not that only, but also lifting up
His hands to heaven." "He suffered without the
gate, in order to shew us that we are not to expect
sanctification from the sacrifices offered within that
city, and that He died not for them only, but for all
mankind;" He lived and suffered upon that Cross till
three o'clock, the time of the evening sacrifice; He,
the One only meritorious Victim, Whom all previous
typical sacrifices had shewn forth, Whose all-sufficient
Death His Church should for ever shew forth till He
come, making the commemoration of that Sacrifice the
central point of her worship, as He upon the Altar of
the Cross is the centre of devotion to Angels and men ;
beheld in glory by one who now stood by His Cross;
"in the midst of the throne and of the four beasts, and
in the midst of the elders,—a Lamb as it had been
slain ," surrounded by the mystic ritual of the heaven
of heavens.   We cannot see Him now in that ineffable
glory, but with St. John we may stand in lowliest
adoration by His Cross, praying that our eyes may be
purged by that sight to behold Him as our Judge, to
rejoice in Him as our eternal and exceeding great
Reward.

"They crucify Him :" those fewest words give to
us an inexhaustible store of meditation, the penitence

• Isa. lxv. 2.   • Rev. v. 6.

and love of His saints has dwelt upon them for nearly two thousand years, and still,—

"Fresh as when it first was shed,
Springs forth the Saviour's Blood."

"Yet have I set My King upon My holy hill of Zion y." The King Who had said, "Let the lifting up of My hands be as the evening sacrifice *." His Throne, the Cross ;—"because also by a tree death had entered, it must needs be that by a tree it should be abolished, and that the Lord, passing unconquered through the pains of a tree, should subdue the pleasures which flow from a tree."

"We still gather round the bed of that beloved King. He is not there now, for He has awaked up after its painful rest." But to us the Cross of the sufferer is the chair of the Master, as we try to remember something of what He suffered for us on that hard couch, to "remember all the words of love He spoke;" "His marvellous works that He hath done, His wonders and the judgments of His mouth *," while thus dying thereon.

For He thought it little to be made man, He must also be rejected of men; little to be rejected, He must be dishonoured too; little to be dishonoured, He must be put to death too; but even this must be too little, it must be by the death of the Cross. We think perhaps at most of what that Death has purchased for us; let me at least to-day dwell on what it cost

y Ps. ii. 6.   * Ibid. cxli. 2.   * Ps. cv. 5.

G

that divine Love, that contrition may be awakened in
my heart, that I may hate those sins which nailed
Thee there.   For how fearful, how unspeakably great
must sin be, when He Who was to make atonement for
it, He Who was to put away all death, chose the ex-
tremest and worst kind of death?   All His whole Body
hanging upon that Cross, breathes love to us, and calls
for our love, and hatred of that which caused the wrathful displeasure of God to go over Him.   His Head is
bent down, His Arms stretched forth, His Bosom
opened to us.   O Priest and Victim, the one High-
Priest, the one Sacrifice, there is no whole part in Thy
Body, all Thy Bones are out of joint, the wrathful
displeasure of God against sin has gone over Thee.
The sins of each one of us,—mine—were amongst
those which weighed Thee down—Thee, Son of God,
being in the Form of God,—Son of Mary, taking upon
Thee the Form of a servant.   When we give way to
evil thoughts, we imagine evil against Him, Who,
having power to take up His Life, and power to lay it
down, willed to lay it down to save us.   When we speak
evil words, swords are in our lips to slay Him[b].
When we do evil actions, we reward evil for good
against Him, and hatred for His love[c].   What could
He have done more than He has done?

     "For it is said to us at this time, 'Behold His Bed,
which is Solomon's[d].'   Behold Him arrayed in purple

[b] Ps. lix. 7.   [c] Ibid. cix. 5.   [d] Cant. iii. 7.

on His Cross for us, no longer the mocking purple of the soldiers, but the victorious purple of His own Blood.

"Who, but the true Solomon, the God of all Wisdom, could have devised for Himself such a resting-place, in the last hours of His mortal life? Who but He could have invented so hidden a counsel by death to destroy death, by laying down life to restore to us everlasting life? Who but the true Solomon, the Prince of Peace, could have made peace between God and man, and that by the agony and shame of this very bed?"

Friday.

FATHER, FORGIVE THEM, FOR THEY KNOW NOT
WHAT THEY DO.

Thy word is a lamp unto my feet, and a light unto my paths.—Ps. cxix. 105.

THEY who listen to Thy words know more and more that "Thy lips drop as the honeycomb; honey and milk are under Thy tongue, and Thy speech is comely ᵉ." "What will be Thy words in the country, if Thou speakest on this sort in the way?" But how can we rightly hearken to, think, speak, meditate of Thy words during those awful hours, when, out of the strong, stronger in death than in life, came forth sweetness? For now the Lamb is "stretched on the most holy altar of the cross, burning in His own fire of love, His arms wide open to embrace every afflicted heart, His eyes fixed on heaven, opening the gates of Paradise hitherto barred by the sin of Adam. And as our Lord is the High-Priest, by Whom we are reconciled and have access to the Eternal Father, and is also the sacrifice most acceptable to God, for the sake of which He forgives the sins of the whole world; He, the Lord, seeing Himself on the altar of the Cross, made the sacrifice of Himself and offered up Himself for the whole human race, with all His will and in the fulness of His love, with an infinite desire for the salvation of all sinners. There He completed the

ᵉ Cant. iv. 3, 11.

reconciliation of sinners with God. There He embraced and united to Himself both heaven and earth, and made of both one Church, one household, and one fellowship."

And as He was then Priest, the One great Priest and Bishop, so with His sacrifice He offers incense, the incense of His holiest prayer, "Father, forgive them, for they know not what they do." He had now brought His gift to the altar, and though He did not and could not seek to be reconciled to His brethren, since no fault had been found in Him, yet He seeks reconcilement for them with His Father. He, the only Teacher, Whose life was greater than His words, ceases not, in mortal agony to teach us, to give us the most perfect pattern of how we should keep His great precept. He had taught us to ask for forgiveness in His own words, and to believe that so asking we shall be forgiven; one only condition He annexed to that forgiveness, that we should forgive others; and now in the act of offering up the sacrifice from which forgiveness and all other benefits should flow to us, He teaches in act what He had taught in words; gives us an example, that we should do as He has done to us. We think it much, for the most part, if, after our anger at any offence is past, we forgive. But His first words after they had pierced His hands and His feet, were of love for His torturers. While we are feeling keenly the pain of any offence we exaggerate its extent, and imagine unkindness which does not exist. He finds an excuse to plead on behalf of those who with every aggravation of cruelty were shedding the blood of the just. "He saw some that were His among many aliens; for those He even then asked pardon, from whom He was then still receiving wrong. For He regarded not that He was dying by their hands, but only that He was dying for them. Much was forgiven them, much done by them and for them, to the intent that no man may despair of the forgiveness of his sin, seeing they obtained pardon who killed Christ. Christ died *for us,* but was He put to death *by us?* But those men saw Christ dying by their wickedness, yet believed in Christ forgiving their wickedness. Until they drank the blood they had shed, they despaired of their own salvation *.*" He prays not for them only, but for all, for me. "Our sins nailed Christ our Lord to the Cross, loaded Him with pains and torments, and offended His eternal Father; but because they have blinded and condemned us, He hath more compassion upon us than upon Himself, and without taking thought for Himself, He prayeth that we may be pardoned as blind and ignorant." "O Love, thou hast thy fullest triumph in this Divine Lamb, doest in Him whatsoever thou wilt." Thou Who art love, shew the glory of Thy power by changing even such a cold, unloving heart as mine, drawing it unto Thee, and teaching it to love others, Thy brethren. Let me not be excluded, since Thou, lifted up, wilt draw all unto Thee.

' St. Augustine.

Saturday.

TO-DAY SHALT THOU BE WITH ME IN PARADISE.

And Samson lay till midnight, and arose at midnight and took the doors of the gate of the city.—JUDGES xvi. 2.

DEATH is close to the Lord of Life, for He would taste death for every man. We cannot doubt that He Whose lovingkindness and mercy follow us all the days of our life, would have said more to satisfy the cravings of love to know something of those who have left us, had it been possible for us to apprehend such knowledge. But the few, fewest words of Holy Scripture as to the departed, the all-but utter ignorance in which we are left, seems to shew us that such knowledge is either impossible to us, or would harm us. We must bear the bitter penance of that desire for knowledge which led to sin, and must endure the agony of ignorance concerning those who have been as our own soul. But He Who was now drawing nigh to the mystery of death, Who made us what we are, and knows our yearnings, gives us from His Cross as much comfort, (may we not believe it?) as we can receive here. For His answer to the prayer of a departing soul is the assurance "thou shalt be with Me." Where the soul of Christ made brief abode, there should be the soul of the penitent thief.

There may we trust the souls of our beloved, knowing
that wheresoever He was, in life or in death, there
it is good for them and for us to be. It is true that
the absolute promise of that blessedness was only
made to one, the firstfruit of His Passion, but may
we not hope that all who, like him, come to Christ in
penitence and faith, have part in his blessedness, since
we know at least that they rest? And "in Paradise."
Round the bitter Cross breathe gales from our lost
Eden, which the Second Adam is about to re-conquer
for us, turning aside the fiery sword. "Going down
into the dark realm of shadows, and returning from it
as a conqueror, having burst like another Samson,
the gates of the city of the grave which shut Him in."
Only let us consider a little what manner of spirit it
was which found such acceptance with Christ, and
pray Him to give us the same. As it is the greatest
instance of mercy which is recorded, so there is no
sublimer instance of faith, hope, charity, humility,
penitence, entire conversion of the heart. Faith, which
acknowledges the thorn-crowned Crucified as King,
as God, as having power over hell and over death,
power to save to the uttermost those that should come
to Him. Hope, that even he with all his sins would
not be cast away. Love, mourning over his Lord's
sufferings, and seeking to convert his fellow-sufferer.
Humility, acknowledging that torture and death is
but the due reward of his deeds. Penitence, shewn
by his acceptance of the punishment of his iniquity.

"As the first to enter Paradise with Christ, he is perhaps set forth as an example of that temper which is required of all who would enter there. For that man has most attained unto evangelical righteousness who is the most thoroughly penitent, the most truly humbled; and all Christian good works lead to this humiliation. For he that hungers most shall be most filled; he that is most abased, shall be most exalted. Here was 'the poor in spirit,' the first to enter into the kingdom; here was one that knocked, to whom the door was opened; here did our Lord afford from the depth of His own anguish, consolation to all dying persons, who shall die in Him and in His faith; here did He afford them most blessed assurance respecting that intermediate state of the good, that whatever it is, it is to be with Him in Paradise."

O King of Glory, Lord of Paradise, True Friend and Shepherd of my soul, in me Thou hast another thief, one whom Thou mightest most justly condemn. I confess that Thou art the King of Paradise, and that Thou canst give it to whom Thou wilt, and that Thou wilt not refuse it to any one who turns to Thee:—

> " Dread Preacher, Who to fathers old
> Didst wonders in the gloom unfold;
> Thy perfect creed O may we learn
> In Eden, waiting Thy return.
>
> They saw Thy day, and heard Thy voice,
> And in Thy glory did rejoice;
> And Thou didst break their prison bars,
> And lead them high above the stars."

G 3

To Him we must thankfully trust the souls that
have left us, desiring for them, in the words of an
ancient Liturgy, and "all who having finished their
course in this life, and having been set free from the
sea of their iniquities, have approached to Thee, our
Father and Brother, according to the flesh in this life,
rest in that spiritual and mighty bosom—the spirit of
joy in the habitations of light and happiness, in the
tabernacles of shade and quiet, in the treasures of
blessedness, whence every sorrow is exiled afar; where
the souls of the pious without any labour await the
firstfruits of life, and the spirits of just men in like
manner look forward to the end of the promised reward—to that region where the labourers and the
weary look towards paradise, and they that are invited
long for the wedding-feast of the celestial bridegroom ;
where they that are called to the banquet wait till they
may ascend thither, and ardently desire to receive that
new garment of glory ; where every distress is banished,
and where joys are found."

Monday before Easter.

WOMAN, BEHOLD THY SON! BEHOLD THY MOTHER!

And He said, Take now thy son, thine only son Isaac, whom thou lovest, and get thee into the land of Moriah; and offer him there for a burnt offering upon one of the mountains which I will tell thee of.—GEN. xxii. 2.

" Now there stood by the Cross of Jesus His Mother ;" for the hour had come of which Simeon spake, when her holy Child should be set for a sign that should be spoken against, of which He had spoken, " ' Mine hour is not yet come* ;' saying, as it were, ' thou gavest not birth to that part of Me which works a miracle; thou gavest not birth to My Divine nature, but forasmuch as thou didst give birth to My weakness, I will recognise thee when that same weakness shall hang upon the Cross.' This, then, was the hour, at that time not yet come, the hour in which it would be right for Him, being at the point to die, to acknowledge her of whom He was in mortal manner born." At the time of His first miracle, " He that created Mary was making Himself known by power, but now

* St. John ii. 4.

that to which Mary had given birth was hanging
on the Cross."

Blessed among all generations, that not only did
she bear Him, but, when His hour came, was found
at the foot of the Cross. Yet what depths of anguish
are contained in those words, " Now there stood by
the Cross of Jesus, His Mother." She, the highly-
favoured one, who had found such ineffable favour
with God,—Virgin-Mother, daughter of her Son,—
she who had borne and nourished Him, stands by to
see Him, Bone of her bone, and Flesh of her flesh, endure such anguish as none ever bore before. And He
suffers the added pain of seeing her anguish. Holy
Scripture is silent as to the thirty years during which
He abode "in meek duty," by her side at Nazareth; all
the unspeakable wonder and veiled glory of that home
are hidden from us ; but we know at least that He
Who came to set us a perfect example, and Who was
Himself the author of filial love, must have so perfectly fulfilled every slightest duty and prompting of
that love, as to make her mother-love the most perfect
which this world has ever seen. If mother's love will
bear with so much of thanklessness and unlovingness in
children, what must have been Mary's love for the "Son
that never did amiss," for the wondrous Child Whom she
knew to be Son of the Highest, the Holy Thing Which
had been born of her, and Who was subject unto her?
Yet now she stands by His Cross. It seems as if in
this world the greater the love, the greater must be

the suffering; she who sang the Magnificat, who
carried in her arms to His Temple the glory of His
people Israel, must endure that the sword should
pierce her bosom. We cannot doubt that as in her
early joy she said, "Be it unto me according to Thy
word," so now in this hour of torture her heart was
"one with His Almighty Will, changed by the o'er-
shadowing Dove," that "looking not on the death of
the Hostage, but on the salvation of the world," she
willingly gave up Him Who had been given to her.

On Mount Moriah of old the holocaust of two
human wills had been offered to God; for "three dim
days of doubt and fear" had Abraham's heart been
wrung, and yet had submitted itself to God; but it
was reserved for a Mother, his blessed daughter, to do
so not only in anticipation, but in consummation of
anguish. On Mount Calvary again parent and Child
unite in offering their wills to the Divine Will.

What shall be her exceeding great reward for ever,
we know not; but even by the Cross she has her
reward; at this supreme hour she is the "sole earthly
care" of her Divine Son; "already suffering as man,
with man's affection He commended her of whom He
was made Man," the Master of the Saints giving an
example of tender filial love and duty, "when, not
as God for the servant whom He had created and was
ruling, but as Man for the Mother of whom He was
born and whom He was leaving, He provided another
to be, in some sort, a son to her in His stead."

Of what great account in God's sight must filial
duty be, when He, accomplishing the most tremendous
act in heaven or earth, wrestling against the sharp-
ness of death,—bruising the serpent's head,—opening
the kingdom of Heaven to all believers, yet takes
thought for the guardianship and care of His Mother.

He, the Perfect Son, never could feel the bitter
pangs of recalling past undutifulness, nor did He
endure the anguish of losing her; her love watched
by His death-bed as by His cradle, yet He can sympathize with such heart-rending grief since He underwent
the greater torture of beholding, without relieving, her
anguish at His pains. She who is nearest and dearest
to Christ must have the nearest part in His Passion,
must be content, like Him, to know that one prayer
could summon to His aid legions of angels, and yet
that He must suffer.

Three women stand by His Cross, "the weaker sex
then appearing the manlier." We are told of such
love and constancy in only one man, and he receives
the dearest legacy from Christ. May we not think
that women may learn an especial lesson from the
part which the Blessed Mother and her companions
took in the Passion of our Lord? He still suffers in
His members, not only in individuals, but in His
Church as a whole, in that Church against which the
gates of hell are ever striving to prevail, trying to
crucify her as they crucified her Lord. The history
of the Church is often the history of a long Passion,

purest and triumphant most when suffering most; and
it seems as if the part of women in this Passion ought
to be mostly like that of the women by the Cross,
—suffering, watching, silence, prayer; not careless
of the troubles of the Church, rather feeling them the
most keenly; not seeking relief by desiring to be
separated from those troubles, content to *do* nothing,
but to suffer and pray much; content even to see the
deep sorrow and suffering of those dearest to them,
"for His Body's sake, which is the Church," and to
be able to do nothing to help or relieve them, to have
nothing to give except love and prayer.

Tuesday before Easter.

MY GOD, MY GOD, WHY HAST THOU FORSAKEN ME?

*And it shall come to pass in that day, saith the Lord
God, that I will cause the sun to go down at noon,
and I will darken the earth in the clear day.—*
AMOS viii. 9.

FROM the sixth hour there was darkness over all
the land until the ninth hour. "Creation could not
bear the outrage offered to the Creator; whence the
sun withdrew his beams that he might not look upon
the crime of these impious men." Moses had once
stretched out his hands towards heaven and brought
darkness upon the Egyptians, while it was light in
the dwellings of Israel; now Christ, the Light which
should lighten every man, stretches out His hands
upon the cross in vain to His own, and "they are
deprived of all light as a sign of the darkness that
should come, and that should envelope the whole
people of the Jews, deprived of the light of God the
Father, the splendour of Christ, and the illumination
of the Holy Spirit."

We feel that we can but adore in silence during
these three hours of darkness, for they have nearly
passed away before the voice of the Beloved is heard
again. And then it is to utter words so mysterious
and awful that we scarcely dare to meditate upon
them or to speak of them. Not to Him is the saying

fulfilled, "The Lord comfort him when he lieth sick upon his bed, make Thou all his bed in his sickness [b];" "but rather in the midst of His unknown sufferings, He cries out, 'My God, My God, why hast Thou forsaken Me.'" We, mere men, cannot know anything of what that cry meant, only we know that "the faith of the Church imbued with Apostolic teaching does not sever Christ that He should be considered as Son of God and not as Son of Man. The complaint of His being deserted is the weakness of the dying man; the promise of Paradise is the kingdom of the living God." Perhaps in this cry He mourned for His own people, "Why hast Thou given Me over exhausted to such sufferings? that the people honoured by Thee may receive the things that they have dared against Me, and should be deprived of the light of Thy countenance." Human nature was forsaken of God because of its sins; and "the Son of God becoming our advocate, laments the misery of those whose guilt He took upon Him, therein shewing how they who sin ought to mourn, when He Who never sinned did thus mourn."

He still teaches us, in His uttermost desolation. He calls Himself forsaken of God, yet does not forsake God. As when in the garden, being in an agony, He prayed *more* earnestly; so now in this mysterious dreadful hour, in agony of spirit and body, He turns to His Father. He teaches us in whatever mental trials to turn *to* God, not *from* Him; to complain

[b] Ps. xli. 3.

to God, not to complain *of* Him. "It is a subject of inexpressible support and consolation, under the weight of the heaviest calamities we can endure; inasmuch as they are not only in themselves exceeding light in comparison, but we have this strong living evidence, that depression of mind and spiritual desertion are no proof of the rejection of God; but rather, like bodily sufferings, form part of that resemblance to His Son, which renders us on that account the more acceptable to our Heavenly Father." If we stand with His faithful ones by His Cross, fixing the eye of faith on that Form fairer than the children of men, yet so marred more than any man, we shall daily learn to draw sweetness and strength from every glance, from every remembrance of His words. We shall feel more vividly year by year—each Lent—that "all these agonies, all these victories, were borne and were gained by One that is mine, by One to Whom I have given myself; but also by One Who has given Himself to me. The bitterness was His, that the everlasting sweetness might be mine: the sickness unto death was His, that the healing might be mine: the weariness and miseries His, that the comfort and refreshment might be mine." And therefore, what depth of love can be sufficient to meet such love? What surrender of every deed, word, thought, fancy, wish, hope, is it not "very meet, right and my bounden duty" to make for Him Who for me bore the desolation of His forsaken humanity?

𝔚𝔢𝔡𝔫𝔢𝔰𝔡𝔞𝔶 𝔟𝔢𝔣𝔬𝔯𝔢 𝔈𝔞𝔰𝔱𝔢𝔯.

I THIRST.

*And David longed, and said, Oh that one would give
me drink of the water of the well of Bethlehem.—
2 SAM. xxiii. 15.*

THE four last words of our Lord must have been
spoken at very short intervals, for we are told that the
first of them, His cry of desolation, was "about the
ninth hour,"—the hour of His death. After that cry,
that awful appeal, that mysterious utterance of the
Son to the Father, He,—close to the consummation,
close to His rest,—returns as it were for a moment to
earth, and, "that the Scripture might be fulfilled,"
· speaks this word, His last to man, "I thirst." He
said it, St. John tells us, knowing that all things were
now accomplished; still to the very end fulfilling the
words, "Lo! I come: I delight to do Thy will, O My
God ᵉ." All the things concerning Himself, in His
mortal life, spoken by Moses and the Prophets, had
been fulfilled, except only this, the vinegar to soothe
His dying thirst. St. Luke records the soldiers coming
to Him and offering Him vinegar, as though they were
frequently doing it in mockery through the hours of

ᵉ Ps. xl. 7, 8.

the Cross; St. Matthew and St. Mark tell us of the
sponge filled with vinegar, and put on a reed, and
given to Him when they supposed that He called for
Elias; and St. John, of the sponge from the vessel full
of vinegar put upon hyssop, and received by Him.

It seems as though all these accounts may either
make mention of one occurrence, or of two, or three.
The reed may have been the stalk of the hyssop mentioned by St. John, or the hyssop may have been bound
on the reed. "We know thus far, that that herb was
prescribed to be used in the Law; it was commanded
to be made use of in sacrifices with scarlet wool, and
considered as purifying. A bunch of hyssop was
dipped in the blood of the Paschal Lamb," and with it
were the lintels and posts marked with the sacrificial
blood. "He was Man apparent, Who was God latent;
He was suffering all these things as He was apparent,
and the Same was disposing all these things as He
was latent." He said, "I thirst;" as much as to say,
"This ye have left undone, give what ye are. For the
Jews themselves were the vinegar, in their degeneracy
from the wine of the Patriarchs and Prophets, and as
it were from a full vessel, filled full of the iniquity of
this world."

Shall we, too, give Him vinegar to drink? When
David, wearied with strife, longed for the water of
his native Bethlehem, there were not wanting three
mighty men to break through the host of the Philis-
tines, and go into jeopardy of their lives to satisfy

his longing; but to David's Son, in His great battle, "when He was thirsty, they gave vinegar to drink." It is spoken of in the Psalms as an additional unkindness. "He indeed bestows upon us the new wine of His blood; we give Him in return a vessel full of vinegar, sourness of heart, and bad affection." Shall we be guilty concerning our Brother, beholding the anguish of His soul, when He besought us, and we would not hear? We cannot but take the very last words spoken to man before His death by our Lord as full of meaning and teaching for each one of us. He knew "that all things were now accomplished, all done and suffered which He had come into the world to fulfil, and, having done all, His last words to us are, 'I thirst.'"

May we say with reverence that He thirsted for some return for this mighty outlay of love; thirsted for our love, obedience, for our salvation; thirsted to see man restored in Him to all which He had lost in the first Adam; thirsted to see of the travail of His soul, and to be satisfied?

"If it is lawful for us so far to press into the mystery of the Passion, of all those griefs which then weighed down our Lord, that surely must have been the hardest and bitterest of all, His fore-knowledge of the obstinacy of those that would not, as He saw by His certain vision, flee for refuge to lay hold on the hope set before them. This is a part of the Catholic Faith, that Christ died, really and truly, by no figure

of speech, for all men; and yet, in the act of dying,
He saw that for them it would be useless.   Job's complaint must have been His: 'Have pity upon me,
have pity upon me, O ye, my friends, for the hand of
God hath touched me.   Why do ye persecute me as
God, and are not satisfied with my flesh?'   Not satisfied with the death I bear for you, as for all; but re-
solved that for you, as not for all, that death should
be in vain."

We desire on the whole to make some return to
His love; we should be shocked to think that His
desire towards us should remain unsatisfied, that we
should reject Him; but do we, do I, each day try to
do something to satisfy the thirst of Jesus for my love;
do I remember how each day tells on eternity; how
each day, by some temptation overcome, some word
unspoken or spoken, some act of duty and love, we
may give a cup of cold water to Him Who thirsts for
it, drawn from that well of water springing up into
everlasting life which He Himself has given us, and
which springs the fresher and purer the more we draw
from it?

The thirst of death!   Thou didst bear it, O most
patient Master, through all those hours of torture,
without complaint, without asking for relief.   As once
in life Thou saidst, "Give Me to drink," that Thou
mightest lead a soul to repentance, so in death Thy
meat and Thy drink is to do Thy Father's Will.   Thou
didst thirst upon the Cross to lead us beside the

waters of comfort during our pilgrimage, to bring us
at last to the "pure river of water of life proceeding
out of the throne of God and of the Lamb [d];" to that
river, "the streams whereof make glad the city of
God [e]."

[d] Rev. xxii. 1.   [e] Ps. xlvi. 4.

Maundy Thursday.

IT IS FINISHED.

His lips like lilies, dropping sweet smelling myrrh.
CANT. v. 13.

"WHAT is myrrh but the bitterness of the Passion, which He endured for us men and for our salvation on Mount Calvary? those priceless drops of Blood which then flowed down on the Cross? that precious ointment on the head of our true Aaron, which ran down His whole Body as He hung on the Tree?"

"Around those lips, where power and mercy hung,
    The dews of death have clung;"

the dew wrung from Him by uttermost torture, which should make the wilderness like the garden of the Lord ; myrrh, "full of bitterness in its purchase, full of comfort and healing in our fruition of it," purifying our corruption, healing our wounds. His lips drop as the honeycomb, for out of the strong came forth sweetness, sweetness in the bitterness of death.

"He doth all things calmly and with power." Now, "because nothing remained that yet ere He died behoved to be done," He said, It is finished. "His humanity having now endured the utmost that it was able, and His love having now attained to the fulfilment of all it had desired; the Divine Love being thus satisfied with the blessings, which, in that Humanity, It had procured for man and for Heaven; and the Human Nature being also satisfied with the fidelity with which It had observed all that had been required of It, and with being made the means of the renovation of Its own nature, the Lord, as one who at last sees the time to be come for gathering the first-fruits of His labours, exclaimed, 'It is finished.' "

They who watched by His Cross must have heard those words with almost a thrill of joy, as many a watcher since has rejoiced in the midst of sorrow when the death-struggle was past. We can mostly do something to relieve, can hold the dying head; but His Mother must stand by His death-bed, and hear the complaint of His forsaken spirit, of His deadly thirst, without being able to succour. But now at last come words of balm, bitter indeed to those who must see Him die, yet "sweet smelling myrrh," not only to them, but to His Church for ever. He had drunk to the dregs the bitter cup which we had mingled for Him; the prophecies were finished; the work which God had given Him to do was finished; His heavenly example and doctrine were finished; His sufferings were finished; the propitiation for the sins of mankind were finished.

To those who, like His earthly friends, watch by Him through this week, these words come with infinite rest and soothing. All which we have been

H

contemplating is finished: one moment more, and the last enemy shall be overcome; He can suffer no more for us; henceforth, "He shall see of the travail of His soul and shall be satisfied[f]." And for us, His work here on earth "is finished." Still must He, having "broken the gates of brass, and smitten the bars of iron in sunder[g]," be raised again for our justification; ascend, leading captivity captive, to receive gifts for us, "wearing our nature still that He may be able to sympathise;" having once assumed it "because Divinity could not have been nailed to the Cross, retaining it still that humanity may see itself exalted to the throne." Still before that throne He manifests Himself a Lamb as it had been slain, shewing forth His death in Heaven as His Church does on earth, speaking sometimes in visions unto His saints, and saying, "I am He That liveth and was dead[h]." But all that He could do for us on earth "is finished;" He, delivered for our offences, has paid their full penalty. We may come to Him as we are, utterly vile and laden with sins, for His warfare for us is accomplished, and the iniquity of His people pardoned. He has left nothing of His redeeming work for us to finish, but in the greatness of His strength, mighty to save, has trodden the wine-press alone. And He, Who came not only to be a sacrifice for sin, but also an ensample of godly life, has given such grace to those forgiven and accepted in Him, that they too

f Isa. liii. 11.   g Ps. cvii. 16.   h Rev. i. 18.

have been able to say, "I have finished my course," "I have fought a good fight[1]." What strength can Jesus, the Author and Finisher of our faith, impart, when His servants, rejoicing in His strength, can speak such words? All is of Him; shewing "the closeness of the relation between the Head and the members; and what He, our King and Lord doth, they do, because He Who did it for them, doth it in them. What they do, they do by the virtue of His might, treading in His steps, walking where He has made the way plain, and by His Spirit."

[1] 1 Tim. iv. 7.

Good Friday.

FATHER, INTO THY HANDS I COMMEND MY SPIRIT.

In the day that thou eatest thereof thou shalt surely die.
                                                GEN. ii. 17.

JESUS must bear the doom of death, that as in Adam
all die, in Him all might be made alive. Yet "when
now nought of suffering remains to be endured, death
still lingers, knowing that it has nothing there. The
ancient foe suspected somewhat unusual. This Man,
first and only, he found having no sin, free from guilt,
owing nothing to the laws of his jurisdiction. But
leagued with Jewish madness, Death comes again to
the assault, and desperately invades the Life-giver."
Jesus dies—for us, for me. Having power to lay
down His life, He lays it down for us. He cried
with a loud voice, "that it might be shewn that the
act is done by power." "Who so sleeps when he
will, as Jesus died when He would? who so lays aside
his clothing when he will, as He put off the flesh when
He would? What must we hope or fear to find His
power when He judgeth, if it was seen to be so great
when He died!" "He did not, when He had expired, bow His Head, as happens with us, but when
He had bent His head, then He expired." He willed
to die, because "He would have it known how great
God's love to man, Who desired rather to be loved

than feared," and "that He might abolish with yet
more justice the sentence of death which He had
with justice passed. For as the first man had by
guilt incurred death through God's sentence, and
handed down the same to his posterity, the Second
Man, Who knew no sin, came from heaven that death
might be condemned, which, when commissioned to
seize the guilty, had presumed to touch the Author
of sinlessness."

Jesus does not forget us in His last words; "for
He commends to His Father through Himself all
mankind quickened in Him; for we are His members;"
teaching us "that the souls of the saints are not
henceforth shut up in hell as before, but are with
God, Christ being made the beginning of this change."

To-day it is hard to think of ourselves at all, to
think even of what His death has purchased upon us,
to do anything but fix our eyes on that Crucified
Form, "set up for an ensign that we, when we are
beginning to wax faint, may look at It and be re-
freshed; that we, when the Amalekites are too strong
for us, may turn our eyes to It, and find the words
fulfilled, 'they that wait upon the Lord shall renew
their strength:' that we, when bitten by the poisonous
serpent of sin, may fix our glance upon it and be
healed." But we know that though He tasted death
for every man, yet we too must die; and it is here
that we shall gain strength and comfort for that hour

—whether for ourselves—or comfort now in the thought of those who have passed through it. The sting of death is sin: but to-day we behold evidently set forth among us, the Lamb of God, That taketh away the sins of the world. And "death, the greatest danger in one sense—is it not the greatest privilege in another?" He that is dead is free from sin. Who would not die to be delivered from the original corruption which clings to us in the body, to know that we can never again offend God, never grieve Him or those whom He loves? Yet the doom *was* laid on us as a chastisement, that last arrow *is* "the sharpest of the Almighty's store;" but if we, fearing to tread so rough a road, faint at the prospect, our help is here, by His Cross. "It is as if He said, 'I Myself, O poor wandering one, I Myself know the roughness of the road by which you must pass. Steep it is, but it leads to no lower a height than the mountain of the Lord's House; rough it is, but it ends in that sea of gold, as it were transparent glass: a thousand briars beset it on every side, but I took of their thorns, and wove them into a crown; dangerous it is, but it ends in that way where there shall be no lion, neither shall any ravenous beast come up thereupon. Take courage, therefore, O My elect one, I went before thee, but I go with thee too.'" Shall not my soul answer Him and say, "Though I walk through the valley of the shadow of death I will fear no evil, for Thou art with

me, Thy rod and Thy staff comfort me. Thou art He
That livest and wast dead, That art alive for evermore,
and That hast the keys of hell and of death."

> " Soul of the Lord so freely breathed,
> And to the Father's hands bequeathed,
> Draw us with hearts' desire to Thee
> When we among the dead are free.

> " Our souls and bodies, Lord, receive
> To Thine own blessed Easter Eve :
> All our beloved in mercy keep,
> As one by one they fall asleep."

Easter=Eve.—Morning.

THE PIERCED SIDE.

*And the Lord God caused a deep sleep to fall
upon Adam, and he slept.*—GEN. ii. 21.

HE slept, because it was not good for him to be
alone, and that out of his opened side might be formed
one to dwell with him in the Eden of delights, one
whose company should be to him the most delightsome
thing in that Eden.

Now the Second Adam, having gone forth to His
work and His labour until the evening, sleeps, that
He may espouse to Himself a Bride, in whose beauty
He might have pleasure,—a Bride, upon whom He
deigns to bestow His own Name; as it is written,
"In those days shall Judah be saved, and Jerusalem
shall dwell safely: and this is the name wherewith she
shall be called, The Lord our righteousness [k]."

The piercing of our Lord's side is only related by
St. John, the disciple of love, the Evangelist of sacramental mysteries,—he who afterwards beheld in vision
"the holy city, new Jerusalem, coming down from God
out of heaven, prepared as a bride adorned for her hus-
band [l]." But his words shew us how great he counted
the mystery which he wrote of: "He that saw it bare
record, and his record is true, and he knoweth that he

[k] Jer. xxxiii. 16.   [l] Rev. xxi. 2.

saith true, that ye might believe [m]." "As if to say, I did not hear it from others, but saw it with mine own eyes. And His record is true, he adds, not as if he had mentioned something so wonderful that his account would be suspected, but to stop the mouths of heretics, and in contemplation of the deep value of those mysteries which he announces."

So in his Epistle he speaks of our Lord as "He That came by water and blood [n];" and of the "three that bear witness in earth, the Spirit, and the Water, and the Blood [o]:" as also his Gospel is especially the gospel of sacramental teaching, and full of allusions to the Sacraments, (his very words being incorporated into the English Office for Holy Communion,) although he does not relate the actual circumstance of our Lord's Baptism, or of the Institution of the Eucharist.

All through this awful week we turn most naturally to the words of elder saints to express our thoughts, fearing lest perhaps we should say anything irreverent or wrong. And if the lifeless form of those they have loved will cause reverence and awe in the most careless, what must we feel while watching by the lifeless Body of One,—

"True God, true Flesh of Mary made,
In a true grave for sinners laid;"

and while meditating on the mysteries accomplished in Him after His Spirit had departed? We shrink from using our own words; it is St. Augustine who says

[m] St. John xix. 35.   [n] 1 St. John v. 6.   [o] Ibid. v. 8.

"that His Side was opened, that therein might, as it were, be thrown wide the door of life, from which the Sacraments of the Church have flowed out, without which there is no entering in unto life which is true life. That blood was shed for the remission of sins; that water tempers the cup of salvation; this gives both laver and drink. In fore-announcement of this it was, that Noe was bidden to make a door in the side of the ark, by which should enter thereinto the living creatures that should not perish in the Flood, by which creatures the Church was prefigured. With regard to this it was, that the first woman was made out of the side of the man as he slept, and was called *Life*, and *Mother of all living*. Significant she was, truly, of a great good before the evil of her transgression. Here the Second Adam with bowed head slept upon the Cross, that thence might be formed for Him a wife, even that which flowed forth from His Side as He slept. O death, by which the dead come to life again! What cleaner than this blood! What than this wound more healing[p]!" And St. Chrysostom, "Not without a purpose, or by chance, did those points come forth, but because by means of these two together the Church consisteth. And the initiated know it, being by water indeed regenerate, and nourished by the Blood and the Flesh. Hence the Mysteries take their beginning; that when thou approachest to that awful Cup, thou mayest so approach, as drinking from the very Side[q]."

[p] Hom. cxx. Oxf. Trans., p. 1047. [q] Ib. lxxxv., p. 762.

O if Jesus,—surrounded by the adoration of the angelic hierarchy, "ten thousand times ten thousand, and thousands of thousands,"—desired with great desire to win to Himself a Bride from redeemed humanity,—without blemish, glorious, not having spot or wrinkle,—a Bride to whom He says, Thou art all fair, My love,—beholding her "perfect through the comeliness which He has put upon her *"—what manner of persons ought we to be in all holy conversation and godliness—we, members of His Bride, and of the Body which for us was pierced ! " Set me as a seal upon Thine heart, as a seal upon Thine arm •." " A cruel engraving, indeed, though exercised on a lifeless body ; but O, how many trem bling souls have since taken refuge in that wound !— have not, like Thomas, desired to thrust their hand into it for the satisfying of their faith, but have hid themselves in it, till the indignation poured out on a wicked world were overpast ! How many doves have sheltered themselves in this secret place of the cleft rock ! How many thirsting multitudes have drunk of the water that issued therefrom and lived !"

* Ezek. xvi. 14.   • Cant. viii. 6.

Easter-Eve.—Night.

Go forth, O ye daughters of Zion, and behold King
Solomon with the crown wherewith his mother
crowned him, in the day of his espousals, and in the
day of the gladness of his heart.—CANT. iii. 11.

WE may have heard the voice of the Church in
these words at the beginning of Lent; and now, indeed, we have beheld Him, the King of Peace, in
royal apparel, crowned, and reigning. In royal apparel, but it is the purple robe of His Blood; crowned,
but with thorns; reigning, from the Cross; in the
day of His espousals, to a Bride only won in death;
in the day of the gladness of His heart,—for He had
accomplished His warfare,—yet a day of trouble, of
rebuke, and of blasphemy. But we may not dwell on
the sorrow without thinking of the joy; our hearts
turn to joy and brightness as naturally as flowers to
sunshine, for our souls yearn after their first happy
estate, and cannot forget that the garden of Paradise
was our first home. God made us for gladness, for
happiness, and if the new Head of our race must needs
be a Man of sorrows, acquainted with grief, He has,
by bearing our griefs, restored joy to us; "joy in sadness," it may be, here, joy greater than that of Eden;
pleasures for evermore at God's right hand where He
has ascended, the First Fruits of our race. So we are

told that "joy" is one of the fruits of the Spirit, Who
came to renew the face of the earth : and so when she
is about to shew forth her Lord's death, the holy
Church throughout all the world says to her children,
Sursum corda. Think not only of the anguish, but of
the reward; not only of the shame, but of the glory;
not only of the Cross, but of the crown. Lift up your
hearts, with angels and archangels, and all the company of Heaven, to Him Who, with the Holy Ghost,
is for ever most high in the glory of God the Father.
Render high praise and gratulation, since whatever
may remain for us to suffer, His Victory is won, His
Sufferings are past, and He is gone to prepare a place
for us.

When the Queen of the East had seen all the glory
and wisdom of Solomon, " the house that he had
built, and the meat of his table, and the sitting of his
servants, and the attendance of his ministers, and their
apparel, his cup-bearers also, and his ascent by which
he went up into the house of the Lord, there was no
more spirit in her [t]." May we not say, in the words
of a holy man, " We, too, shall see the wisdom of our
Solomon there, for we cannot understand it now: the
marvellous manner in which He has guarded us
through so many dangers, and guided us in so many
difficulties, and made all things—even the most ad-
verse—work together for our good, until He has set
us before Himself. We shall see the 'house that He

[t] 2 Chron. ix. 3, 4.

has built,'—that house not made with hands, eternal
in the heavens : that house, too, of living stones,
which, with such patience, He fashioned in this world
to be His spiritual dwelling in the next. We shall
see the meat of His table, where we shall hunger no
more, neither thirst any more; for the Lamb, Which
is in the midst of the throne, shall feed us, and lead
us unto living fountains of waters. We shall see the
' sitting of His servants,'—the depth of their peace ;
when they shall lie down, and none shall make them
afraid : when, as the Solomon of old spake, there
shall be neither adversary nor evil occurrent. We shall
see ' the attendance of His ministers,'—how they go
on their errands, how they rest not day nor night,
saying, Holy, Holy, Holy, Lord God Almighty. We
shall see 'their apparel,'—that fine linen, clean and
white, which is the righteousness of Saints, those
crowns of gold they wear on their heads, those harps
of gold which they hold in their hands. We shall see
' His cup-bearers,'—those who stand nearest to the
everlasting throne; His Virgin-Mother, the Cheru-
bim that are perfect in knowledge, the Seraphim
that are on fire with love. Those seven things—the
types in the palace of the earthly Solomon—the Queen
of Sheba saw, but when she came to the eighth,—
' his ascent by which he went up to the house of the
Lord,'—then there was no more spirit in her. And
so of us. When we come to the eighth thing, which
speaks of the New Creation as accomplished, to the

octave which fills up the measure of that perfect harmony, the ascent by which we fully, and for ever, ourselves, enter into the very Holy of Holies,—when that
Head which, for us, bowed down upon the Cross, shall
then, in the Beatific Vision, kiss us with the kisses of
His Mouth,—then, indeed, there will be no more spirit
in us. Every power of love will be filled. Then shall
Rachel leave her father's house and its labour for the
true land of Canaan; then Mary Magdalene shall be
called in her own name by the lips of her own dear
Lord; then shall Esther go in to the true Ahasuerus,
shall see his golden sceptre. held out to her, shall
touch it, and shall live for ever."

" Jerusalem, Jerusalem, God grant I once may see
    Thy endless joys, and of the same partaker aye to be.
    Thy houses are of ivory, thy windows crystal clear,
    Thy tiles are made of beaten gold :—Oh, God, that I were there!
    Then shall my sorrows have an end, when I thy joys shall see :
    O my sweet home, Jerusalem, would God I were in thee!"

ERRATA.

P. 44, line 7 from bottom, *for* repentance *read* suffering.
—— line 9 from bottom, *for* feelings *read* failures.

BOOKS AND TRACTS FOR PAROCHIAL USE

JAMES PARKER AND CO.,

OXFORD, AND 377, STRAND, LONDON.

Tales, Allegories, Poetry, &c., suitable for Presents and Reward Books, from 1d. to 2s. 6d.

Seléne ; or, The Queen of the Fairy Cross. 4d.

The Loaves and Fishes. 4d.

Old Christmas. 6d.

Mount Gars ; or, Marie's Christmas-Eve. 6d.

Rhymes and Pictures from Pocci. 6d.

Little Footprints on the Old Church Path. *Fourth Edition.* 8d.

Smyttan's Florum Sacra. 16mo. 1s.

The Matin Bell. 1s.

The Garden of Life ; an Allegory. 1s.

The Poachers. *Second Edition.* 1s.

Ann Ash. Sewed, 1s.

The Child's Christian Year, *New and Cheaper Edition,* 1s.

Woodleigh; or, Life and Death. 2s.

The Christian Year. Cloth, 1s. 6d. ; cheap roan, 2s.

The Lyra Innocentium. Cloth, 1s. 6d.; cheap roan, 2s.

Tracts for Cottagers, (from the Parochial Tracts). 2s.

The Pastor of Wellbourn. Cloth, 2s.

Footprints on the Sands of Time. Cloth, 2s. 6d.

Seven Fairy Tales, *with Illustrations.* Cloth, 2s. 6d.

Ada's Thoughts; or, The Poetry of Youth. 2s. 6d.

The History of our Lord in Easy Verse. 2s. 6d. Coloured, 3s. 6d.

The Singers of the Sanctuary. 2s. 6d.

Parochial Tales, (from the Parochial Tracts). 2s. 6d.

The Two Homes, by the Author of " Amy Grant." 2s. 6d.

The Pilgrim's Progress, (for the use of Members of the Church of England). *Illustrated.* 2s. 6d. Best Edition, 3s. 6d.

Speculation : a Tale. Cloth, 2s. 6d.

The Californian Crusoe. A Mormon Tale. Cloth, 2s. 6d.

The Scholar and the Trooper. Cheaper Edition, sewed, 2s. 6d.

COXE'S CHRISTIAN BALLADS.

Dreamland. 1d.
Hymn of Boyhood. 1d.
England. 1d.
Lenten Season. 1d.
Chronicles. 1d.
Chimes of England. 1d.
Churchyards. 1d.

Little Woodmere. 1d.
Matin Bells and Curfew. 1d.
St. Silvan's Bell. 1d.
Daily Services. 1d.
The Calendar, and "I love the Church." 1d.
The Set in Packet, 1s.

SEVEN FAIRY TALES, *Illustrated.*

1. Little Ino C. and his Companions. 4d.
2. Ulric and Laura. 4d.
3. Sholto and his Little Dog Bowowsky. 4d.
4. Rose and the Fairy Helpful. 4d.
5. The Fairy Devoirgilla. 4d.
6. Sansouci and his Sister Soigneuse. 4d.
7. Bonnatura. 4d.

TALES FROM THE PAROCHIAL TRACTS, *Illustrated.*

26. Alice Grant. 2d.
152. Bye and Bye. 2d.
19. Complaints and their Cure. 2d.
66. The Curate's Daughter. 2d.
83. The Day that never came. 2d.
135. Edward Elford. 2d.
18. Edwin Forth. 2d.
25. Fair on Whit-Monday. 2d.
90. Hannah Dean. 2d.
10. Harry Fulton. 2d.
101. The Hop Picker. 2d.
78. Her Sun has gone down while it was yet Day. 2d.
80. It might have been Worse. 2d.
11. Joseph and his Brethren. 2d.
39. Jane Smith's Marriage. 2d.

149. Little Geoffrey. 2d.
48. Mary Fisher. 2d.
63. Mr. Sharpley. 2d.
141. The Modern Martyr. 2d.
84. Nothing Lost in the Telling. 2d.
89. The Prodigal. 2d.
88. The Promised Estate. 2d.
118. Richard Reveley's Legacy. 2d.
12. The Rock and the Sand. 2d.
85. Too Old to be Questioned. 2d.
9. "Thou shalt not Steal;" or, The School Feast. 2d.
82. Tony Dilke. 2d.
81. The Cloud upon the Mountain. 2d.

THE COTTAGER'S SERIES, (from the Parochial Tracts,) *Illustrated.*

1. The Cottage Pig-stye. 2d.
2. Keeping Poultry no Loss. 2d.
3. Mrs. Martin's Bee-hive. 2d.
4. The Honest Widow. 2d.
5. The Village Shop. 2d.
6. Who Pays the Poor-rate? 2d.
86. Mrs. Morton's Walk. 2d.
148. Twopence for the Clothing Club. 2d.
159. The Widower. 2d.

TALES AND ALLEGORIES from the PENNY POST, *Illustrated.*

TALES FOR THE YOUNG MEN AND WOMEN OF ENGLAND.

1. Mother and Son. 1s.
2. The Recruit. 1s.
3. The Strike. 1s.
4. James Bright, the Shopman. 1s.
5. Jonas Clint. 1s.
6. The Sisters. 1s.
7. Caroline Elton ; or, Vanity and Jealousy. 6d.
8. Servants' Influence. 6d.
9. The Railway Accident. 1s.
10. Wanted, a Wife. 1s.
11. Irrevocable. 1s.
12. The Tenants at Tinkers' End. 1s.
13. Windycote Hall. 1s.
14. False Honour. 1s.
15. Old Jarvis's Will. 1s.
16. The Two Cottages. 1s.
17. Squitch. 1s.
18. The Politician. 1s.
19. Two to One. 1s.
20. Hobson's Choice. 6d.
21. Susan. 4d.
22. Mary Thomas ; or, Dissent at Evenly. 4d.

HISTORICAL TALES ILLUSTRATING THE CHIEF EVENTS IN ECCLE-SIASTICAL HISTORY, BRITISH AND FOREIGN.

1.—THE CAVE IN THE HILLS; or, Cæcilius Viriáthus.
2.—THE EXILES OF THE CEBENNA; a Journal written during the Decian Persecution, by Aurelius Gratianus, Priest of the Church of Arles ; and now done into English.
3.—THE CHIEF'S DAUGHTER; or, The Settlers in Virginia.
4.—THE LILY OF TIFLIS : a Sketch from Georgian Church History.
5.—WILD SCENES AMONGST THE CELTS.
6.—THE LAZAR-HOUSE OF LEROS : a Tale of the Eastern Church in the Seventeenth Century.
7.—THE RIVALS : a Tale of the Anglo-Saxon Church.
8.—THE CONVERT OF MASSACHU-SETTS.
9.—THE QUAY OF THE DIOSCURI : a Tale of Nicene Times.
10.—THE BLACK DANES.
11.—THE CONVERSION OF ST. VLADI-MIR ; or, The Martyrs of Kief : a Tale of the Early Russian Church.
12.—THE SEA-TIGERS : a Tale of Mediæval Nestorianism.
13.—THE CROSS IN SWEDEN ; or, The Days of King Ingi the Good.
14.—THE ALLELUIA BATTLE ; or, Pelagianism in Britain.
15.—THE BRIDE OF RAMCUTTAH : a Tale of the Jesuit Missions to the East Indies in the Sixteenth

16.—ALICE OF FOBBING ; or, The Times of Jack Straw and Wat Tyler.
17.—THE NORTHERN LIGHT : a Tale of Iceland and Greenland in the Eleventh Century.
18.—AUBREY DE L'ORNE ; or, the Times of St. Anselm.
19.—LUCIA'S MARRIAGE ; or, The Lions of Wady-Araba.
20.—WOLFINGHAM ; or, The Convict-Settler of Jervis Bay : a Tale of the Church in Australia.
21.—THE FORSAKEN ; or, The Times of St. Dunstan.
22.—THE DOVE OF TABENNA; and THE RESCUE : a Tale of the Moor-ish Conquest of Spain.
23.—LARACHE : a Tale of the Portu-guese Church in the Sixteenth Century.
24.—WALTER THE ARMOURER ; or, The Interdict : a Tale of the Times of King John.
25.—THE CATECHUMENS OF THE COROMANDEL COAST.
26.—THE DAUGHTERS OF POLA : a Tale of the Great Tenth Persecu-tion.
27.—AGNES MARTIN ; or, The Fall of Cardinal Wolsey.
28.—ROSE AND MINNIE ; or, The Loyalists : A Tale of Canada in 1837.
29. DOBES DE GUALDIM : a Tale of

THE PENNY POST, in volumes.

Vol. I. 1851, to Vol. IV. 1854, 12mo. cl. 1s. 6d. each.
Vol. V. 1855, to Vol. XXI. 1871, 8vo., sewed, 1s. ; cloth, 1s. 8d.
each.

THE CHRISTIAN YEAR.

Fcap. 8vo.—Cl., 7s. 6d.; mor. | 32mo.—Cl., 3s. 6d.; mor. plain,
10s. 6d.; best mor., 15s.; ant. | 5s.; best morocco, 8s. 6d.
cf., 14s | Cheap—Cl., 1s. 6d.; bound, 2s.
18mo.—Cloth, 6s.; morocco, 8s. 6d. |

Facsimile of First Edition, 2 vols., 12mo., boards, 7s. 6d.

TALES, POETRY, &c., suitable for Presents, from 3s. to 10s.

SHORT READINGS FOR SUNDAY SCHOLARS. Fcap. 8vo., cloth, 3s. 6d.
COXE'S CHRISTIAN BALLADS, complete. 3s.
Chronicles of Camber Castle. Cloth, 8s.
Tales and Allegories, (from the Parochial Tracts). 3s. 6d.
RICKARD'S Poems. Fcap. 8vo., 3s. 6d.
KENNETH; or, The Rear-Guard of the Grand Army. Fifth Edition, Illustrated. 5s.
The Silver Bells: an Allegory. Small 4to., cloth, 5s.
For Life: A Story in Two Parts. By LOUIS SAND. Crown 8vo., cloth, 6s.
KEBLE'S Psalter. Fcap. 8vo., 6s.
The LYRA INNOCENTIUM. Fcap. 8vo., 7s. 6d.
KEBLE'S Miscellaneous Poems. Fcap. 8vo., 6s.
Some Years After. Fcap. 8vo., 7s.
Atheline; or, The Castle by the Sea. 2 vols., 9s.
Mignonette: A Sketch. 2 vols., 10s.

SACRED PRINTS FOR PAROCHIAL USE.
PRINTED IN SEPIA, WITH ORNAMENTAL BORDERS.

The Set, One Shilling; or *each*, One Penny.

1. The Nativity.
2. St. John Preaching.
3. The Baptism of Christ.
4. Jacob's Dream.
5. The Transfiguration.
6. The Good Shepherd.
7. The Tribute-Money.
8. The Preparation for the Cross.
9. The Crucifixion.
10. Leading to Crucifixion.
11. Healing the Sick.
12. The Return of the Prodigal.

COTTAGE PICTURES FROM THE OLD TESTAMENT.

A Series of Twenty-eight large folio Engravings, brilliantly coloured by hand. The Set, 7s. 6d.

COTTAGE PICTURES FROM THE NEW TESTAMENT.

A Series of Twenty-eight large folio Engravings, brilliantly coloured. The Set, 7s. 6d.

N. B. Upwards of Eight Thousand Sets of these Cottage Pictures have already been sold. They are recommended by the National Society, in whose "Monthly Paper" appeared a series of lessons on Holy Scripture especially adapted to this series of Prints.

A CATECHETICAL SERIES,

Designed to aid the Clergy and School Teachers in Catechising. Uniform in size and type with the "Parochial Tracts."

I. Catechetical Lessons on the Creed. 6d.

II. Catechetical Lessons on the Lord's Prayer. 6d.

III. Catechetical Lessons on the Ten Commandments. 6d.

IV. Catechetical Lessons on the Sacraments. 6d.

V. Catechetical Lessons on the Parables of the New Testament. Part I. Parables I.—XXI. 1s.

VI. Part II. Parables XXII.—XXXVII. 1s.

VII. Catechetical Notes on the Thirty-nine Articles. 1s. 6d.

VIII. Catechetical Lessons on the Order for Morning and Evening Prayer, and the Litany. 1s.

IX. Catechetical Lessons on the Miracles of our Lord. Part I. Miracles I.—XVII. 1s.

X. Catechetical Lessons on the Miracles of our Lord. Part II. Miracles XVIII.—XXXVII. 1s.

XI. Catechetical Notes on the Saints' Days. 1s.

XII. Catechetical Lessons on Miscellaneous Subjects. 1s. 6d.

The above Set complete in 2 vols., cloth, price 10s.

Part XIII. Catechetical Lessons on the Book of Common Prayer. By the Rev. Dr FRANCIS HESSEY, Author of the "Catechetical Notes on the Parables" and on "the Miracles," in the same ser.es. Papers I. to X., *Introduction, &c.* 6d.

Part XIV. Catechetical Lessons on the Book of Common Prayer. Papers XI. to XXXIII., *Morning and Evening Prayer.* 1s.

Part XV. Catechetical Lessons on the Book of Common Prayer. Papers XXXIV. to XLIV., *Litany, &c.* 6d.

Parts XVI., XVII., XVIII., XIX, XX., XXI. Catechetical Lessons on the Book of Common Prayer. Papers XLV. to CIX., *Collects, Epistles, and Gospels, &c.* Price 6d. each Part.

Part XXII. Catechetical Lessons on the Book of Common Prayer. Papers CX. to CXXVII., *Saints' Days.* Price 1s.

DEVOTIONAL SERIES OF THE PRACTICAL CHRISTIAN'S LIBRARY.

Uniform, in 18mo., limp blue cloth.

1. A Kempis' Imitation of Christ, 1s.
2. Andrewes' (Bp.) Devotions, 1s.
3. Augustine's Confessions, 1s.
4. Cosin's(Bp.)Devotions,&c. 1s.
5. Ken's Manual of Prayers, with Catechism, and Directions, 1s.
6. Sherlock's Self-Examination and Holy Communion, 1s.
7. Sherlock's Meditations and Prayers, 1s.
8. Spinckes' Devotions, 1s.
9. Sutton's Disce Vivere, 1s.
10. ——— Disce Mori, 1s.
11. Taylor's (Bp.) Holy Living, 1s.
12. ——— Holy Dying, 1s.
13. ——— Golden Grove, with Selection of Offices and Prayers, 1s.
14. Wilson's Lord's Supper, 1s.
15. ——— Sacra Privata, 1s.
16. ——— Maxims of Piety, 1s.

FOR DEVOTIONAL USE.

Meditations for the Forty Days of Lent. 18mo., cloth, 2s. 6d.

RIDLEY's Every-Day Companion. The Two Parts in One, price 3s. Or separately, PART I. Advent to Whitsuntide. 2s. PART II. Whitsuntide to Advent. 1s. 6d.

A Daily Text-Book for the use of School-children, &c., sewed, 6d.

Hours of Prayer; being Devotions for the Third, Sixth, and Ninth Hours. With a Preface. Sixth Edition, Royal 32mo., vellum, 1s.

Horæ Sacræ. Royal 32mo., cloth, 2s. 6d.

SANDFORD's Vox Cordis. 2s. 6d.

MANT's Dial of Prayer. 1s.

The Seven Penitential Psalms, in large type, 2d.

129. Seven Meditations on the Life of our Lord. 9 for 1s.

164. Meditation on the Day of Judgment. 50 for 1s.

Spiritual Communion. Devotions from the works of Bps. PATRICK and WILSON. 32mo., 4d.

Helps to Daily Self-Examination. 1d. each.

57. Meditation. 12 for 1s.

Helps to Prayer and Devotion. Crown 8vo., cloth, 8d.; sewed, 4d.

A Portuary for the Laity. Long Primer 24mo., limp cloth, 2s. 6d.; limp morocco, gilt edges, 5s.

——— 32mo., limp cloth, 6d.; cloth, 9d.; morocco, 1s. 6d.

——— ——— thick paper, morocco, 2s.

——— ——— With Hymns and Introits, limp cloth, 1s. 6d.

——— 48mo., red rubrics, limp russia, 2s. 6d.

Daily Steps towards Heaven. Roan, gilt edges, 2s. 6d.

——— In large type. Square 8vo., cloth, 5s.

PRIVATE PRAYER.

Books of Private Prayer—continued.

204. Daily Prayers for the use of those who have to work hard. 12 for 1s.

Bp. Ken's Manual of Prayers for Winchester Scholars. Best Edit. 1s.

—— Manual of Prayers, adapted to general use. 6d.

8. Morning and Evening Prayers for Young Persons. 50 for 1s.

7. Morning, Evening, and Midnight Hymns. 25 for 1s.

143. Morning and Evening Hymns for a Young Person. 50 for 1s.

Prayers for the Little Ones, by E. C. P. 16mo., 3d.

Morning and Evening Prayers and Hymns for Elder and Younger Children. On a Card. 1d. each.

GRESLEY'S Help to Prayer, in Six Tracts. 12mo., 1s.

105. On Private Prayer. 25 for 1s.

MARRIOTT'S Hints on Private Devotion. 12mo., 1s.

Prayers for Persons associated in aid of Missions. 1d. each.

An Itinerary, or Prayers for all that Travel. 6d.

Devotions for a Time of Retirement and Prayer for the Clergy. As used in the Diocese of Oxford. Fcap. 8vo., cloth, 1s.

CARTER (Rev. T. T.) CLEWER MANUALS.

Part I. Daily Offices of Prayer, and other Devotions. 24mo., 1s.

Part II. Hours of Prayer, Litanies, &c. 24mo., cloth limp, 1s.

Part III. Instructions and Devotions for Adult Baptism and Confirmation. 24mo., cloth limp, 1s.

Part IV. Repentance. 24mo., cloth limp, 1s. 6d.

Part V. No. 1. Instructions on the Holy Eucharist. 18mo., paper covers, 1s.

FAMILY PRAYER.

BELLAIRS' Prayers for Christian Households. New Edition. 1d.

Liturgia Domestica: Services for every Morning and Evening in the Week. Third Edition. 18mo., 2s. Or in two Parts, 1s. each.

EARL NELSON'S Family Prayers. With Responsions and Variations for the Different Seasons, for General Use. Separately, Paper Covers, 3d. each; with the Psalter, cloth, 9d.

Also, The Calendar of Lessons; A Course of Reading for the Christian Year, for Private or Family Use. Cloth, 6d.

The Family Prayers, with the Psalter and a Calendar of Lessons, for the Use of the Master. Cloth, 1s. Fourth revised Edition.

Short Forms of Family Prayer, by a Layman. Fcap. 8vo., cl. 2s. 6d.

178. Daily Office for the use of Families. 9d.; cloth, 1s. 2d.

142. Morning and Evening Family Prayers. 18 for 1s.

Short Manual of Daily Prayers for every Day in the Week. 6d.

111. Litany for Ember Weeks. 18 for 1s.

78. On Family Prayer. 50 for 1s.

FOR SCHOOLS AND COLLEGES.

99. Prayers for Schoolmasters and Schoolmistresses. 50 for 1s.

THE HOLY SCRIPTURES.

HOOK's Proper Names in Holy Scripture accented. 2s.

COTTON's Obsolete Words in the Bible. 6d.

JONES (of Nayland) on the Figurative Language of Holy Scripture. Cloth, 1s. 6d.

74. The Right Way of Reading Scripture. 18 for 1s.

A Plain Commentary on the Book of Psalms. (Prayer-book Version.) Chiefly grounded on the Fathers; for the Use of Families. 2 vols., Fcap. 8vo., cloth, 10s. 6d.

The Psalter and the Gospel. The Life, Sufferings, and Triumph of Our Blessed Lord, revealed in the Book of Psalms. A Selection of the most striking Parallel Passages contained in the Psalter and the Gospel. Fcap. 8vo., cloth, 2s.

"In this small tract the author has exemplified the fact, that the name of David is substituted, throughout the Book of Psalms, for that of our Blessed Lord; and he has, from that rich mine of Christian theology, 'shewn the life, sufferings, and triumph of our Blessed Lord, revealed in the Book of Psalms.'"

Key Words to the Psalter; being Short Anthems, or Antiphons, proper to each Psalm. Reprinted from the "Penny Post." 8vo., 3d. each.

A PLAIN COMMENTARY ON THE FOUR GOSPELS. By the Rev. J. W. BURGON, M.A. A New Edition. In 5 vols., limp cloth, 21s.

Catechetical Lessons on the Parables of the New Testament. Part I. Parables I.—XXI. 1s.

Part II. Parables XXII.—XXXVII. 1s.

Catechetical Lessons on the Miracles of Our Lord. Part I. Miracles I.—XVII. 1s.

Part II. Miracles XVIII.—XXXVII. 1s.

A Harmony of the Gospels, from "Daily Steps." 32mo., 2d.

DOWNING's Short Notes on St. John's Gospel. Intended for the Use of Teachers in Parish Schools, and other Readers of the English Version. Fcap. 8vo., cloth, 2s. 6d.

DOWNING's Short Notes on the Acts of the Apostles. Uniform with

THE PRAYER-BOOK.

Catechetical Lessons on the Prayer-book. *See p. 5 of this Catalogue.*

Catechetical Lessons on Morning and Evening Prayer, and Litany. 1s.

A Companion to the Prayer-book, compiled from the best sources. 1s.

Abp. LAUD on the Liturgy. 16mo., 2s.

HAKE's Holy Matrimony.—Devotional Exercises. 2d.

SALKELD's Godly Sincerity of the Common Prayer-book Vindicated. 6d.

Questions on the Collects, Epistles, and Gospels, throughout the Year. Pt. I. Edited by the Rev. T. L. CLAUGHTON. Fourth Edition, 2s. 6d.

———— Pt. II. Fourth Edition. Cloth, 2s. 6d.

BEAVEN's Catechism on the Articles. 1s. 6d.

Catechetical Lessons on the Thirty-nine Articles. Sewed, 1s. 6d.

WENHAM's Questions on the Collects. 1s.

147. Love your Prayer-book. 25 for 1s.

Ten Reasons why I Love my Prayer-book. 12 for 3d.

THE CATECHISM.

The Catechist's Manual. With Preface by the BISHOP OF WINCHESTER. Third Edition. Crown 8vo., cloth, 5s.

An Outline of the Church Catechism. Royal 8vo. In a Tabular form. 1s.

Grandmamma's First Catechism. By a Lady. Fcap., 4d.

NICHOLSON'S Exposition of the Catechism of the Church of England. A New Edition. 1s. 6d.

CHEERE's Church Catechism Explained. Cloth, 2s. 6d.

SHERLOCK's Paraphrase of the Church Catechism. 18mo., 6d.

Progressive Exercises on the Church Catechism. By the Rev. HENRY HOPWOOD, M.A.

Parts 1, 2, and 3. Analytical Exercises. 2d. each.

Part 4. Biblical Exercises. 2d.

The Catechism adapted for the Use of those who have not been Baptized. 1d.

HENSLEY's Steps to Understanding the Church Catechism. 1d. each.

THE LORD'S PRAYER.

Catechetical Lessons on the Lord's Prayer. 6d.

176. The Lord's Prayer. 25 for 1s.

THE CREED.

1. Exposition of the Apostles' Creed. 9 for 1s.
186. Questions and Answers on the Athanasian Creed. 16 for 1s.
184. Letter from a Clergyman on the Athanasian Creed. 9 for 1s.
125. THE CHIEF TRUTHS: I. The Holy Trinity. 25 for 1s.
183. II. Incarnation. 25 for 1s.
184. III. Passion. 25 for 1s.
43. IV. Resurrection. 25 for 1s.
44. V. Ascension. 25 for 1s.
45. VI. Judgment. 25 for 1s.
217. VII. Holy Ghost. 18 for 1s.
218. VIII. Holy Catholic Church and Communion of Saints. 18 for 1s.
219. IX. Forgiveness of Sins. 25 for 1s.
220. X. Life Everlasting. 18 for 1s.

The Chief Truths, *containing the above* 10 *Tracts*, cloth, 1s.
Catechetical Lessons on the Creed. 6d.

THE TEN COMMANDMENTS.

209. I. Thou shalt have none other Gods but Me. 50 for 1s.
210. II. Thou shalt not make to thyself any Graven Image. 50 for 1s.
211. III. Thou shalt not take the Name of the Lord, &c. 50 for 1s.
131. Swear not at all. 50 for 1s.
5. IV. How to spend the Lord's Day. 18 for 1s.
130. Where were you last Sunday? 25 for 1s.
212. V. Honour thy Father and Mother. 50 for 1s.
166. VI. Thou shalt do no Murder. 25 for 1s.
213. VII. Thou shalt not commit Adultery. 50 for 1s.
69. The Unmarried Wife. 18 for 1s.
214. VIII. Thou shalt not Steal. 50 for 1s.
215. IX. Thou shalt not bear False Witness. 50 for 1s.
72. Truth and Falsehood. 12 for 1s.
216. X. Thou shalt not Covet. 50 for 1s.
The Ten Commandments, *containing the above* 14 *Tracts*, *cloth*, 1s.
Catechetical Lessons on the Ten Commandments. 6d.

BAPTISM.

The Gift of the Holy Ghost in Baptism and Confirmation. 32mo. 3d.
Holy Baptism. An Earnest Appeal to the Unbaptized. Sewed, 1d.
200. The Baptismal Service for Infants explained. 9 for 1s.
187. Holy Baptism. 9 for 1s.
120. Friendly Words on Infant Baptism. 12 for 1s.
175. Questions about Baptism answered out of Scripture. 18 for 1s.
56. Registration and Baptism. 18 for 1s.
185. Why should there be God-Parents? 25 for 1s.
102. Choice of God-Parents. 50 for 1s.
103. Advice to God-Parents. 25 for 1s.
169. Who should be Sponsors. 50 for 1s.
Baptism, *containing the above* 9 *Tracts*, *bound together in neat cloth*, 1s.
VAUGHAN'S Doctrine of Baptism, &c. 1s.

CONFIRMATION.

190. The Confirmation Service explained. 12 for 1s.
 28. Questions for Confirmation. First Series. 12 for 1s.
 29. Ditto. Second Series. 12 for 1s.
 30. Preparation for Confirmation. 25 for 1s.
100. A Few Words before Confirmation. 25 for 1s.
 91. Hints for the Day of Confirmation. 50 for 1s.
158. Catechism on Confirmation. 18 for 1s.
 27. A Few Words after Confirmation. 12 for 1s.

Confirmation, *comprising the above 8 Tracts, in bright cloth*, 1s.
Questions before Confirmation. 50 for 1s.
HOPWOOD'S Order of Confirmation, illustrated. Third Edition.
 Cloth, 2s. 6d.
Confirmation (Parochial Papers, No. XII.) 1s.
NUGEE'S Instructions on Confirmation. 18mo., 1s.
Confirmation according to Scripture. 3d.
Notes on Confirmation. By a Priest. Sewed, 6d.
Short Catechism on Baptismal Vow and Confirmation. 2d.
ARDEN'S Lectures on Confirmation. 1s.
VAUGHAN'S Doctrine of Baptism and Laying on of Hands. 1s.
LOWNDES' Preparation for Confirmation. 16mo., cloth, 1s. 6d.
KARSLAKE'S Manual for those about to be Confirmed. Second
 Edition. Crown 8vo., sewed, 1s.

THE LORD'S SUPPER.

Devotions before and after Holy Communion. Fourth Edition,
 16mo., cloth, 2s.
———— With the Order of the Administration of the Lord's
 Supper. 16mo., cloth, 2s. 6d.
193. The Lord's Supper. 9 for 1s.
 76. Plain Speaking to Non-Communicants. 18 for 1s.
106. One Word More to Almost Christians. 25 for 1s.
 77. The Lord's Supper the Christian's Privilege. 25 for 1s.
189. Have you ceased to Communicate? 18 for 1s.
183. Am I fit to receive the Lord's Supper? 25 for 1s.
196. Have you communicated since your Confirmation? 18 for 1s.
192. A Persuasive to frequent Communion. 18 for 1s.
206. Devotions preparatory to the Lord's Supper. 18 for 1s.

The Lord's Supper, *comprising the above 9 Tracts, bound in cloth*, 1s.
What is Unworthy Receiving? 1 Cor. xi. 29. 1d.
CLAUGHTON'S Duty of Preparing for the Lord's Supper. 1d.
Catechetical Lessons on the Sacraments. 6d.
Spiritual Communion, (from Patrick and Wilson). 4d.
LAKE'S Officium Eucharisticum. New Edit. Cloth, red edges, 1s. 6d.

DOCTRINE OF THE CHURCH.

WORDSWORTH'S Credenda: A Summary of the Apostles' Creed. 4d.

KEBLE's Selections from Hooker. 18mo., 1s. 6d.

VINCENT OF LERINS against Heresy. 18mo., 1s. 6d.

PYE's Two Lectures on the Holy Catholic Church. 12mo., 1s. 6d.

JONES' (of Nayland) Tracts on the Church; containing, An Essay on the Church, A Short View of the argument between the Church of England and the Dissenters, The Churchman's Catechism, On Private Judgment, A Private Admonition to the Churchman, The House of God the House of Prayer. Cloth, 1s. 6d.

JONES' Essay on the Church. Fcap. 8vo., 1s.

A Plain Argument for the Church, on a card. 1d.

124. A Scripture Catechism on the Church. 4d. each.

155. A Catechism concerning the Church. 9 for 1s.

197. Are all Apostles? or, The Christian Ministry. 25 for 1s.

Ten Reasons why I Love my Church. 12 for 3d.

A few Plain Testimonies in favour of Episcopacy. 4 pp., 8vo., ½d.

THE SEASONS OF THE CHURCH.

21. How to spend Advent. 50 for 1s.

22. How to keep Christmas. 25 for 1s.

23. New Year's Eve. 18 for 1s.

52. How to keep Lent. 18 for 1s.

53. Ken's Advice during Lent. 25 for 1s.

126. Tract for Holy Week. 9 for 1s.

168. Tract for Good Friday. 18 for 1s.

163. How to keep Easter. 25 for 1s.

59. Neglect of Ascension-Day. 50 for 1s.

174. How to keep Whitsuntide. 50 for 1s.

Catechetical Notes on the Saints' Days. 1s.

A SIMPLE CATECHISM on the SEASONS of the CHURCH, explained by the History of the New Testament. For the use of Children in Schools. In wrapper, price 3d., or 2s. 6d. per dozen.

THE TRACTS FOR THE CHRISTIAN SEASONS. A Series of sound religious Tracts, following the order of the Sundays and Holy-days throughout the year. 4 vols., 12s.

A SECOND SERIES of the above under the same editor, and chiefly by the same writers. 4 vols., 10s.

A THIRD SERIES of the above. Edited by the Rev. J. R. WOODFORD. 4 vols., cloth, 14s.

SHORT SERMONS FOR FAMILY READING, following the Course of the Christian Seasons. In Sixpenny Parts; or the Set complete, containing Ninety Sermons, 2 vols., Fcap. 8vo., cloth, 8s.

PUBLIC WORSHIP.

CAPARN's Meditations in Church before Divine Service. Sewed, 6d.

Reasons for Staying Away from Church. Reprinted from the "Penny Post." 8vo. 3d. per dozen.

The Congregation; its Duties, (Parochial Papers, No. X.) 1s.

The Fabric of the Church, (Parochial Papers, No. VIII.) 1s.

Reverence in Church. On a Card. 3d.

203. On Common Prayer. 50 for 1s.

13. Be in Time for Church. 25 for 1s.

55. "No Things to go in." 25 for 1s.

207. The Gate of the Lord's House. 9 for 1s.

108. What do we go to Church for? 12 for 1s.

20. How to behave in Church. 25 for 1s.

181. Conduct in Church. 18 for 1s.

67. On saying Responses in Church. 25 for 1s.

68. Do you Sing in Church? 25 for 1s.

145. Daily Common Prayer. 18 for 1s.

3. Do you ever Pray? 50 for 1s.

51. No Kneeling, no Praying. 18 for 1s.

137. A Word to the Deaf about coming to Church. 50 for 1s.

71. Church or Market. 25 for 1s.

65. Beauty of Churches. 25 for 1s.

153. Doors or Open Seats. 12 for 1s.

47. Plain Hints to Bell-Ringers. 25 for 1s.

113. Church Choirs. 25 for 1s.

150. Plain Hints to a Parish Clerk. 25 for 1s.

151. Plain Hints to Sextons. 50 for 1s.

179. Plain Hints to an Overseer or Guardian of the Poor. 50 for 1s.

199. Plain Hints to a Churchwarden. 18 for 1s.

The Church of the People. Monthly, 1d.

The Canticles, Pointed for Chanting, by S. ELVEY. Fcap., sd., 6d.

The Psalter, Pointed for Chanting, with Explanations and Directions. By the late STEPHEN ELVEY, Mus. Doc. Sixth Edition. Fcap. 8vo., limp cloth, 2s. 6d.

The Anglican Hymn-Book. Edited by the Rev. R. C. SINGLETON, M.A., and E. G. MONK. Mus. Doc. Fcap. 4to., cloth, 5s.

———— Super-royal 18mo., cloth, 2s. 6d.

———— Words and Treble Part, square 16mo., cloth, 1s. 6d.

SICKNESS AND AFFLICTION.

BRETT's Thoughts during Sickness. Cheap Edition, 1s. 6d.

ARDEN's Scripture Breviates. Cloth, 2s.

LE MESURIER's Prayers for the Sick. 3s.

Verses for the Blind and Afflicted. Fcap. 8vo., 6d.

The Order for the Visitation of the Sick. Fcap. 8vo., sewed, 1d.

15. Sudden Death. 50 for 1s.

121. Make your Will before you are Ill. 50 for 1s.

32. DEVOTIONS FOR THE SICK. Part I. Prayer for Patience. 12 for 1s.

    33. Pt. II. Litanies for the Sick. 12 for 1s.

    34. Pt. III. Self-Examination. 12 for 1s.

    35. Pt. IV. Confession. 18 for 1s.

    36. Pt. V. Prayers for various occasions. 12 for 1s.

    37. Pt. VI. Prayers for Daily Use during a long Sickness. 12 for 1s.

    38. Pt. VII. Devotions for Friends of the Sick. 12 for 1s.

    39. Pt. VIII. Ditto.—When there appears but small Hope of Recovery. 25 for 1s.

    40. Pt. IX. Thanksgiving on the Abatement of Pain. 12 for 1s.

    41. Pt. X. Devotions for Women "Labouring with Child." 12 for 1s.

    42. Pt. XI. During time of Cholera, or any other general Sickness. 25 for 1s.

75. Hints for the Sick. Part I. 12 for 1s.

116. Ditto. Parts II. and III. 9 for 1s.

31. Friendly Advice to the Sick. 12 for 1s.

96. Scripture Readings during Sickness. 18 for 1s.

112. Are you better for your Sickness? 25 for 1s.

94. Will you give Thanks for your Recovery? 25 for 1s.

107. Form of Thanks for Recovery. 50 for 1s.

64. Devotions for the Desolate. 50 for 1s.

172. Devotions for Widows. 50 for 1s.

70. Thoughts of Christian Comfort for the Blind. 18 for 1s.

136. Patience in Affliction. 18 for 1s.

14. To Mourners. 12 for 1s.

Devotions for the Sick. *containing a selection of the above Tracts*

MISCELLANEOUS.

ACLAND'S Precautions against Cholera. 30 for 1s.
———— Health, Work, and Play. 6d.
A Parting Gift for Young Women leaving School for Service. 4d.
The Prevailing Sin of Country Parishes. ½d. each.
No Nearer to Heaven. 1d.
140. A Word in due Season to the Parents of my Flock. 18 for 1s.
62. A Word of Exhortation to Young Women. 12 for 1s.
160. An Exhortation to Repentance. 25 for 1s.
93. A Clergyman's Advice to a Young Servant. 12 for 1s.
97. To Masters of Families. 25 for 1s.
165. A Word to the Aged. 25 for 1s.
156. Examine Yourselves. 18 for 1s.
157. A Few Words on Christian Unity. 12 for 1s.
98. To Sunday School Teachers. 12 for 1s.
61. To Parents of Sunday Scholars. 25 for 1s.
177. A Word to the Pauper. 25 for 1s.
95. Farewell Words to an Emigrant. 25 for 1s.
16. A Few Words to Travellers. 50 for 1s.
188. The Farmer's Friend. 18 for 1s.
79. A Few Words to the Farmers. 3d. each.
194. Thou God seest me. 25 for 1s.
60. A Word of Warning to the Sinner. 25 for 1s.
92. A Word of Caution to Young Men. 12 for 1s.
182. Now is the Accepted Time. 50 for 1s.
144. Never mind : we are all going to the same place. 25 for 1s.
170. "Too Late." 12 for 1s.
87. Shut Out. 25 for 1s.
119. Flee for thy Life. 25 for 1s.
49. Be sure your Sins will find you out. 25 for 1s.
110. The Tongue. 18 for 1s.
24. Think before you Drink. 25 for 1s.
195. Why will ye Die ? 50 for 1s.
146. Twelve Rules to live by God's Grace. 50 for 1s.
104. The Christian's Cross. 25 for 1s.
122. Consult your Pastor. 25 for 1s.
117. Reverence. 25 for 1s.
58. Schism. 12 for 1s.
109. Conversion. 18 for 1s.
4. Almsgiving every Man's Duty. 9 for 1s.
50. Weekly Almsgiving. 18 for 1s.
188. Honesty, or Paying every one his Own. 9 for 1s.
117. Sailor's Voyage. 18 for 1s.
162. Evil Angels. 18 for 1s.
180. The Holy Angels. 18 for 1s.

PERIODICALS.

TRACTS FOR THE CHRISTIAN SEASONS: being Readings for every Sunday and Holyday in the Year.

———— FIRST SERIES. Edited by BISHOP ARMSTRONG. 4 vols., cloth, 12s.

———— SECOND SERIES. 4 vols., cloth, 10s.

———— THIRD SERIES. Edited by the Rev. JAMES RUSSELL WOODFORD, M.A., Vicar of Kempsford, Gloucestershire. 4 vols., Fcap. 8vo., cloth, 14s.

THE PENNY POST. A CHURCH OF ENGLAND ILLUSTRATED MAGAZINE, issued Monthly. Price One Penny.

Each number consists of Thirty-two Pages 8vo., printed on toned paper, with several Illustrations, and contains Tales, Stories, Allegories, Essays Doctrinal and Practical, Correspondence, &c. The object is to combine amusement with instruction; to provide healthy and *interesting* reading adapted for the Village as well as the Town.

Monthly—One Penny.

Subscribers' Names received by all Booksellers and Newsmen.

*** *Arrangements can be made, by application to the Publishers, for* LOCALIZING *this Magazine.*

PARKER'S CHURCH CALENDAR AND GENERAL ALMANACK contains, besides the usual information of an Almanack, much that is contained in no other, particularly with regard to the state and progress of the Church in America and the Colonies. Crown 8vo., price 6d. *Issued annually.*

DIOCESAN EDITIONS FOR 17 DIOCESES, 1s. each, *annually.*

MISCELLANEOUS.

STRONG CALICO LENDING WRAPPERS for the Parochial Tracts, with tapes, &c. 1d. each.

DR. ACLAND'S FORMS FOR REGISTERING THE SANITARY CONDITION OF VILLAGES. 8vo., 50 in wrapper, 1s. 6d.; 100 in

www.ingramcontent.com/pod-product-compliance
Lightning Source LLC
Chambersburg PA
CBHW030605040726
47497CB00008B/2862